Since the Accident

Since the Accident

Jen Craig

PUNCHER & WATTMANN

First published in 2023
Published by Puncher and Wattmann
PO Box 279
Waratah NSW 2298

https://www.puncherandwattmann.com
web@puncherandwattmann.com

ISBN   9781922571632

Cover design by Bettina Kaiser
Typesetting by Morgan Arnett
Printed by Lightning Source International
First published by Ginninderra Press in 2009

 A catalogue record for this work is available from the
NATIONAL LIBRARY OF AUSTRALIA   National Library of Australia

For S, Z and J

I

I had already been back in Australia for some weeks but it wasn't until the second of May that I got around to visiting my sister Trude to see how she had been since the accident. I was the only one in the family she would listen to, as our mother kept telling me, and so it was important that I put in the effort if I didn't want to be responsible for losing her.

As it had been nearly a decade since I had been in the country and I still didn't dare to drive on the left-hand side of the road, I hadn't yet bought a car. The moment I arrived, I settled into a room in one of those central city hotels in Chinatown, a hotel which turned out to be ten minutes' walk from the first English language school to give me a contract. I walked to the English language school and back again in the afternoon five days a week. Everything I needed for my new life in Australia could be met within a half-hour walking radius of a room with small, chill, south-facing windows looking out onto a shadowed mess of roofs and high walls: this view a relief after that clear Sydney light which makes the smallest details too perfectly visible.

To get out to Kogarah, to the cramped hotel room, as I had heard from our mother, where Trude had moved herself to without thought as usual to the long-term consequences, all I would need to do was to catch a train in the opposite direction (the other direction, of course, being towards our mother in Pymble). The trains were more frequent now, our mother had told me, although she couldn't vouch for the other routes. She'd heard the timetable was available on the Internet, so I could always look it up. Kogarah wasn't so far away. Not as far away as it had been in France.

I'd been expecting all this cajolery and wheedling. Cajolery and wheedling were what I'd grown up with, but despite my best efforts to ignore their effects on me, it still took some weeks to get past that instinctive resistance to our mother, and her efforts to persuade me, to make that otherwise very simple journey out into the suburbs to visit my sister, and all this on top of the many months that had passed since I had first heard the news about the accident, which from the perspective of now, of this point of writing after her sudden departure for the hills near Mittagong, is extraordinary.

By coming home to Australia, and more specifically to the city in which I had grown up, I had intended that the relationship between my sister Trude and me should revert to how it had been for us in our teens. Even before the accident happened, I had fantasised about how proximity to not only Trude but to all of our family might have made something different of my relationship to them and, as a direct consequence, or so I had explained to my friend Remi on a number of occasions, to myself. I had fantasised about seeing more of my sisters, about seeing more of my parents and the various now elderly relatives I remembered visiting when I was a child and a teenager. By seeing more of my parents and my sisters and my relatives I would be able, or so I had explained, to become a more connected person.

I heard of Trude's accident while still living in France. I had been working late at the language school when a fax had come in, the words written in our father's distinctive hand, crammed up against the top of the page so as to save on space: *Your sister Trudy has had serious accident. Come home immediately. Love Mum and Dad.* It was impossible, of course, to return at that notice. I had already used up my leave and good graces at the school by being unwell for several weeks too many earlier on in the autumn, and when I rang one of my other sisters the following day, it was clear that the urgency wasn't as great as our father had made out. Trude's first operation had been successful and, although a second operation was necessary, there was every reason to expect, I heard, that she would continue to live.

Every now and then I would receive another fax or letter (our parents never used email) and so I learned that, after she had recovered sufficiently from the second operation and was well enough to return home, Trude had been busy, as is well known among the family – too busy to answer phone messages or emails. It was just as well, too, that I had not flown back to Sydney in those early months, because then I was very easily able to keep out of the way of the relationship that had blossomed very romantically, or so I had heard, since the accident. I kept out of their way, which is to say that, quite unintentionally, I did what any loving sister would have done. It was only a pity, I occasionally thought, that I hadn't got round to seeing her before the relationship, as one of my sisters put it, took her over. It made me doubt for a while that it was possible ever to go back, as I said to Remi, to really return to the person I had been.

No sooner, though, had her recovery gone smoothly (a miraculous recovery, as one of my other sisters had said), her relationship blossoming as much as the recovery itself (the two of them – the recovery and the blossoming relationship – making it all the more difficult, or so it seemed then, for me to visit her as I'd planned) – no sooner had all this happened than I received a fax from our mother saying that everything had changed. No longer was Trude taking miraculous strides. She had left the relationship. It was a concern, our mother had written, because she simply wasn't listening to anyone at the moment. Trude would not listen to any of her other sisters. To the rest of our family she was deaf and dumb. I was the only one, or so our mother had written, whose opinion she had ever valued. I needed to see her. I needed to talk her into moving back, if not back into the relationship, at least out of the old room in the pub she had moved herself to, that old room in a pub being not a place, certainly, for someone in her condition.

When I arrived in Sydney, I didn't want to be specific about when I would go and visit Trude. I was busy, I told our mother, too busy to go for a little while yet. I had only just arrived in the country, I said. I was too far down on the casual list at work to be relaxed about taking days off, and on the weekend I was still (as I told our mother) on the look out for permanent accommodation.

And yet I did take that train out to Kogarah not so many weeks later. In doing this, I told myself, not only was I pushing past that instinctive reaction to our mother – an instinctive reaction that has always made me worry about my capacity to live as a rational being – but I was actually going out to visit my sister, the sister whom I'd always valued and who had apparently always valued me.

In Kogarah, I wasted some time around the station, dithering around what shops I could find both above the station and in the main street leading away from it. I had intended to go into a bookshop and find something inspiring about an artist for this sister whom I valued – since I'd gathered from our mother that she'd found her art again – but I hadn't reckoned on the impossibility of finding a bookshop in Kogarah. There were the occasional newsagents, a supermarket over the station; two-dollar shops sprouting plastic baskets and chairs on both sides of the main street. Circling back to the cluster of two-dollar shops right over the station itself I found a poor selection of remaindered fantasy novels from which I selected something that was at least the first in a series: a book about a Celtic warrior nun who retires to a scriptorium and becomes involuntarily drawn into the life of another warrior nun whose life she has pledged herself to copying.

When buying a bunch of separately wired gerberas from a small florist shop several blocks down the street, I was asked whether I was visiting a relative. At first I was alarmed at the apparent transparency of what I was doing until I remembered that there was a large public hospital in the area, one that Trude might still have been going to now and then.

The pub Trude was staying in was in fact very close to the station and a little up the hill in the other direction. I almost walked past it, so closed up and dark it looked from the outside. Pushing open one of the doors, I found myself in a bar mutely jangling with a horse race mounted high in one corner. The bar was empty, or so I thought, until I saw a small silhouette against the neon squares of a cigarette machine on the other side of the room. For a moment I thought that the owners had let a child truant through its doors, a child who was bent over some unfinished homework or doodling, and yet I also recognised something in the energy of that hand. It was Trude writing – either writing or drawing – and it looked as if she was using the light from the cigarette machine to see what she was doing.

I didn't want to startle her, so I allowed myself to be careless in my approach. Even so, she didn't look up, or at least not until the last moment when, in the same movement, she turned over what she was working on and slipped it into a battered-looking cardboard wallet folder in front of her. She looked at me and seemed to manage a half smile, and so, without knowing what else to do, I went up to her and, with the awkwardness that comes from having grown up in a family where nobody has ever showed physical affection, I bent down and kissed her cheek, and then laid my gifts of the gerberas and the fantasy novel too quickly in front of her. I started apologising for the kind of book I had chosen. Trude turned over the book to read what was written on the back of it. Apart from raising her eyebrows, as if to acknowledge a shared opinion on the quality of this sort of fantasy novel, she seemed neither to be pleased that I had brought her this book as a present, nor particularly displeased. As for the gerberas, her fingers went out to fiddle with the wired stems.

Sometimes, when we were children, she used to fiddle with things or draw when I went into her room to talk to her. She would listen to me but at the same time she would fiddle or draw.

I asked whether I should ask someone for a jug of water for the flowers, but she said that it was OK, which I took to mean that she would rather I didn't. I pulled out a chair and sat at the table opposite her.

I asked what she'd been drawing, but she didn't want to say. She was still in the early stages of a very new idea, she said, and from recent experience she thought it was better to keep her ideas to herself. When other people could see what you were doing they quickly developed a stake in what you did.

As it was so dark in the empty bar, I couldn't imagine what she had been observing for her drawing. I turned round and looked in the direction that she might have been looking. All I could see were the empty tables and chairs and the windows in the doors looking out onto the street. Perhaps she'd been drawing the furniture, I thought, or the people who hadn't yet arrived. Trude had always liked drawing people, I remembered.

Trude then began telling me about the convenience and friendliness of the pub. It was so convenient living here; everything was at her feet, so to speak. Through those doors (and she nodded towards the one I had come through), she could step out onto the street and hail a taxi with only a minimum of effort. People, she said, had the wrong idea about pubs. Some people thought only drunks and losers hung around places like this. Those people were wrong. They had completely the wrong idea. She had never encountered as much friendliness as she had while living here. For convenience and friendliness, she wouldn't go past a pub like this any day. Not only were the other patrons very friendly, but the owners were too. In fact, if she wanted a drink, she said, she needn't go to the bar because all she had to do was raise her hand like this (she demonstrated) and Charlene would come over to ask what she wanted. They were used to her being here, even when no one else had arrived because it was too early in the day. Charlene and Dennis were familiar with her habits. Usually Trude only went up and down the stairs from her room once in twenty-four hours. This way she could avoid having to use the stairs too often. Charlene and Dennis knew this, but they weren't people who made a fuss about things. They were normal people, the most normal in the best sense of the word.

Some people thought that Charlene and Dennis were somehow lesser kinds of people simply for the fact that they ran a pub and made no pretensions about it. These same people would judge Charlene, Trude thought, for the fact that she wore poly-cotton stretch knits and K-Mart jewellery, and had two piercings in each ear as had become fashionable in the 'eighties. Charlene and Dennis lived above the pub in their own separate accommodation and some nights they invited Trude into their flat to watch *Big Brother* or a *Simpsons* special. They would never dare to judge her and so she could never judge them. If she sometimes accepted their invitations to watch *Big Brother*, it was only that she wanted them to know that she didn't despise what they liked to watch. Quite the opposite: accepting their invitations to watch *Big Brother* was a way of stepping away from her old life towards a more normal and friendly kind of existence.

Still fiddling with the gerbera stems, Trude then said in a lower voice that she knew why I was there. Our mother had warned her that I was coming to see her. No doubt our mother had told me to say that she needed either to move back in with Murray, which was impossible, or to move somewhere closer to our parents (even in with our parents), which she didn't want to do either.

She said she might as well tell me first-up that she had no intention of moving away from the pub at the moment. Charlene and Dennis had become her friends, and they were looking after her better than anyone else could. Charlene used to be a nurse and still did the occasional shift up at Accident and Emergency at the hospital here. Charlene was a very experienced nurse and both of them were good cooks (they did pub meals on weekdays). Dennis had done up her room so that it was easy and practical. Trude only paid Charlene and Dennis the usual amount but they were always going out of their way to make sure she was all right.

Trude then asked whether I wanted a drink and, before I could reply, she held up a hand and a broad blonde woman with a stretch purple top came over to the table. When this woman took our orders, she remarked on how alike Trude and I were: as alike as a pair of twins. Perhaps she was hoping that Trude might have introduced us, but Trude kept running her fingers down the stems of the gerberas.

A little later, after we'd had our drinks, Trude then told me that in fact she was glad I had come to visit her in the pub. She said nothing at this point about my years of absence from the country, acting instead as if it had been only a matter of weeks since we'd both sat together in similar circumstances. She'd been having a few issues with our mother, she said. Before the accident it had been sort-of OK. Trude's promotion at work and then those few moments of fame when she had been interviewed on Radio National had made our mother deliriously happy. Although it was dangerous, she said, when our mother was deliriously happy, it had at least made it easier to resist her criticisms – criticisms for the fact that she hadn't yet got married and still dressed in the sloppy way of people who are on the dole; for the fact that she hadn't yet bought anything on the real estate market but was continually pouring money, like a fool, into the pockets of strangers – this promotion and fame both strengthening her own position and seeming to weaken our mother's. But all that was in the past now, all that forgotten.

Since the accident, she said, the issues had changed. She was being treated like a child. For no reason, and without an iota of permission from herself, our mother was making decisions for her and speaking of her best interests.

The difference now, Trude said, was the constant phone calls (because, after all, what else could she be doing with her time?). The meddling with her doctors and other people she had to deal with. Trude had turned off her mobile for long periods of the day, but she couldn't stop our mother from ringing her doctors. When she got angry with our mother over this, our mother only said that she was protecting Trude and her best interests and would get angry in return, saying that Trude didn't seem to be too bothered about looking after herself.

Trude told me that since she had moved to the pub she had spent long hours in this downstairs bar trying to think through the events of the last several months. It didn't help that people, and our mother in particular, had already decided on an agenda for her. Trude had made the first move on her own that she had been able to since the accident and already there had been a response that was out of all proportion to what she had done. She had moved out of Murray's place, but she hadn't moved far (did I know that Murray actually lived only a few streets away?). She had done nothing drastic. In fact, for the first time she was doing what our mother had been at her to do for months: she was getting back into her art. All these months since the accident our mother had been at her and at her about her art. It would be so useful for her recovery, she'd been saying to Trude, and such a great distraction.

Of course, when Trude had been a child, she now reminded me, our mother hadn't wanted her to be an artist at all. Trude had wanted to be an artist and to go to art school but our mother wouldn't hear of it. Being an artist wasn't a career, our mother would say. It wasn't a career, it was only a hobby. Now take the law, she would say: studying law would at least ground her in something substantial. Trude would have been a good barrister, our mother had said, since she'd always been good at arguing her case. You can always come back to art, she had said then, the coming back to art only meant to be an addendum to a degree in law and (hopefully) a marriage that had been effected while studying or working in the law. Look at Grandma Moses, our mother would say, referring to a little white-haired old lady who had recently been in magazines along with her bright, naïve canvases. Doing law won't mean that you give up your art forever.

The fact that Trude had dropped the law and turned the arts part of her degree into a social work degree had angered our mother. Anybody, she had said to Trude, can be a social worker. And then, when Trude had given up the social work for public relations: anybody can fool anybody else into spending money.

This had been what had happened and what our mother had always said, but since the accident, Trude told me, she'd had a very different story. Since the accident, and more particularly since Trude had moved in with Murray, our mother had talked as if she'd only ever encouraged her daughter to pursue her art. Our mother said she'd never been dead against her art per se. She had only been trying to protect her daughter and encourage her to keep it in proportion to other more important things. Trude, very typically, had only ever wasted her opportunities, our mother kept saying. She could have been a barrister, but instead had gone and got that nothing job that anyone could do. She had even been talented in art, but all she had done was throw it away. And so looking at the logic of her arguments, Trude said, our mother should have been happy that her daughter was getting back into her art again. She couldn't understand our mother. She couldn't understand her at all.

I had to realise, Trude now told me, that it wasn't very easy taking this step in the name of her art. If she hadn't been so sure of how she felt, she would have only decided to get back into her art in secret. The last thing that she wanted our mother to think was that she had been right all along and had only needed to get through to Trude. This was the way that our mother always talked about us. Our mother knew what was right and we were just stubborn and stupid because we refused to listen to her. In the light of this history then, it was very difficult to actually choose to do whatever it was that our mother wanted from us. All of our instincts were against it, our most deep-seated instincts.

In the end, Trude told me, her decision to get back into her art had to be more important than her issues with our mother. Everything was conspiring against her doing what our mother had said and yet, as it turned out, by following her own heart and taking one step at a time, she had ended up deciding to do the very thing that she might otherwise have not wanted to do on account of our mother. It was nothing short of miraculous – that overused word which for the first time could readily be applied to her situation, she thought.

Everyone had been using this word since the accident. It drove her mad how, from the very first hours she was conscious, the word 'miraculous' had insinuated itself into everything people said about her: her survival despite the amount of blood she had lost and the number of broken bones; her ability to get movement happening in her feet; the new man in her life who had also been her saviour. And yet the way Murray had been able to persuade her to go on that Getaway Art Workshop I might have heard about – against all her instincts of self-preservation – his success in getting her to go at all was nothing short of miraculous.

Trude picked at the raffia encasing the wires that were wound around the stems of the gerberas. She had to tell me about Murray. No doubt our mother had already told me a lot about Murray, but it was important that I emptied my mind of what our mother had told me and looked at things as they really were. Her getting together with Murray was quite another story in itself, she said. From what our mother might have told me, I could well be imagining someone very different to how he was. These days, said Trude, she could understand if I thought that Murray was the right-hand man of our mother, but that was far from being fair to him. He was nothing like our mother. Everything about him was different to our mother. The workshop had been a gift from him and that was the only way he had ever talked about it. The whole point of the workshop had been to take the opportunity to immerse herself in her art, he'd said. For the first time in her life she was to be thinking about herself and her art and not about her work or her obligations to anybody or anything. He had wanted to foster this interest in art and this was going to be his gift. In fact, he had seen it as a crying shame that she had never done anything with her art other than entertain her colleagues at any workplace she had been in with her caricatures of various members of that workplace. He had been astounded that, for all her adult life, she had never once taken her art as seriously as it should have been taken, and as she was still on an extended sick leave from work and had the payout from the accident, what better use of her convalescence than to spend it thinking about herself and doing relaxing and constructive things?

Murray had found the art workshop up north on the Internet and, before even mentioning it to her, he had gone ahead and booked her a place on the three-day workshop. When he had told her about it, he had done it with such confidence, such presumption. It was during one of those routine household activities, she remembered. Perhaps she had been helping him unpack some shopping he'd placed high on a bench for her. Perhaps she had just gone into the kitchen to see what he was cooking. At first she hadn't quite understood what he had said to her. In fact, she had thought he was talking about her physiotherapy (he was a physiotherapist himself). They were always talking about her physiotherapy sessions.

As soon as she realised that Murray had booked her on a Getaway Art Workshop – booked her on the course without consulting her at all – she had been so shocked at what he'd done that she had burst into tears. Since the accident, I had to understand, tears had come to her very easily. All it took was for a distraught mother on the television news to say the simplest thank you to everyone who had helped her look for her little Louise, and Trude would be choking. The soundtracks in movies, too, affected her badly. While on the one hand she found herself becoming more inured to the building tension of movie thrillers (before the accident, she would never have been able to sit in the same room as the stalking of a victim), on the other hand, during the more romantic scenes, where the hero or heroine realised what they had been missing in their lives all these years – when they looked out with longing over a beautiful landscape – the build-up of emotion in the soundtrack was unbearable and she would find herself unable to speak.

The roller coaster of sound and visuals in a film had become too much. She would be elated in the hair-flying scenes, touched in the forgiveness dialogues – so elated and touched and eventually wrung out that, even as she felt the tears coursing down her face, her nose growing thick with vicarious distress, she would be furious that she had let herself succumb to what only seemed a series of cold-blooded calculations on the filmmaker's part. She would be furious at herself and also at the film that had been made, it seemed, for the sole purpose of dragging these degrading tears from her face. She was disgusted at how her body – this same body which had hung on to itself despite the major trauma of a near fatal accident, whose crushed bones and damaged organs had held fast to themselves with the mute intelligence of unfamiliar and even superior life forms for so many hours and weeks and months – how this same body reacted now to what could only be interpreted as meaningless tear-ringing experiences.

And so when her body reacted to Murray's gesture of buying her a place at this Getaway Art Workshop without consulting her, it was humiliating for her first reaction to have been tears. Instead of reading her tears as a sign of anger or even shock, he had read them for how they must have seemed to be whenever they watched the television in his lounge room: a perhaps very fitting response to what he obviously felt was a thoughtful and generous offer (this she could tell by the way he had looked back at her with the tears brimming at his own lids, by the smile that kept undulating gently – irritatingly – across his face).

In the end, of course, she had to be grateful for what he had done for her, but at the time it was not only a matter of appearing to be grateful (her tears had already done that), but in her confusion, her own mouth seemed to take on the task of saying what he must have hoped to hear from her, her mind lagging behind with both wonder and disgust. She was amazed, quite blown away, she had said. She wondered how on earth he could have known about her art. She kept reiterating this wonder at his knowing and talked of his thoughtfulness. She worried openly about what the workshop would be like – would it be difficult and would she be good enough? He had been pleased, she thought, that she voiced such doubts.

In fact, once she'd grown used to the fact that he had already paid for the Getaway Art Workshop with his own credit card and that her repeated suggestions that he ring up and cancel it were taken as no more than what he might have expected from her – those token gestures of protest which made the giving only sweeter – she stopped talking about it at all for some weeks, so angry (with both herself and Murray) and anxious, that she could not trust herself to say the words that might have begun at last to disentangle what had just occurred. And yet for all her anger and anxiety, she said, it was different to the anger that she might have shown our mother had our mother dared to do such a thing. Our mother would never have sent her on a course, she knew. It wasn't our mother's style. Our mother would have rung her up to harangue her about a course, never leaving her alone but always trying to persuade her. With Murray it was different. He might instead have bought her a large and useless golden clock. You could hate the clock, she said, but at least he wasn't going to try to persuade you to like it. He would set it up for a while in some prominent place, with all the stubbornness of someone who has learned that saying nothing for a while does occasionally work, but after a week or so the clock would have disappeared. That was how Murray was. He was different to our mother.

All the same, Trude said, she had eventually felt very nervous – or if not exactly nervous, anxious and stressed about going on the art workshop. It was inevitable, she knew, that there would be all sorts of people there, people she was sure she couldn't face. Some would have only recently taken up art to assuage some kind of midlife crisis – the kinds of people who had never really drawn and who couldn't draw for nuts. It would have driven her mad, she said, to be in a situation where there were all these beginners and hopeless amateurs wrestling with their muddy or overly naïve palettes, with the teachers walking around (as they would be) praising the students' work even though it wouldn't deserve any praise – these beginners and hopeless amateurs being praised because it helped with their self-esteem. And, what was more, she imagined them all having to start with drawing oranges and bananas and labouring over a colour wheel as she had done once at high school. She knew that it would have driven her completely mad if it had turned out like that. The other possibility was that there might have been people who were equally untalented but who had been in the lucky position that they hadn't had to work for a number of years and as a consequence had been able to spend a lot of time doing below-standard work – the kind of people who would look down on somebody else who hadn't had any exhibitions or didn't work at their art full-time.

All these anxieties, she told me, were not new anxieties. Every time she had ever thought of doing an art course at TAFE or joining a life-drawing class, there had been the same fears. They weren't the general fears that anyone might have, anyone who one day might have thought about joining an art class. She would play little scenes in her head: the frustration of drawing clear glass jars, the pointed distraction of a teacher, and all the time she would be aware of a sound not unlike the ticking of a watch as if it was only there, in such an art class, that time and its opportunities would slip away from her. She saw herself as drawing or painting madly just to keep up with this ticking. Only by not going to such a workshop would she be able to still the sound of it and live as if she were living in a potentially endless interval between the acts of that perhaps more real world (where there was always that ticking).

And so, she said, her body had betrayed her – this inexplicable betrayal after all that had happened to it – and without being able to confront the issue of Murray's cheek, she just let each day carry her forwards to the date of the workshop. She thought of its arrival with a grim fearlessness, as once she might have anticipated the kinds of operations she'd only recently had to undergo.

At least, though, for the month or so beforehand she had been able to get around the house without a stick. This had heartened her because she didn't want people to feel sorry for her at the workshop, and nor did she want people to think that she was only doing the workshop for post-accident therapy. While she knew that Murray must have only thought of its

22

therapeutic relevance, and no doubt had had the idea placed in his head by her mother (who had already used this argument to her face), she was determined not to let anybody know about what had happened to her because she knew that then she would start receiving those little insincere, encouraging comments she had always despised when she'd heard them being offered to others. She wanted nobody to notice how painful it was for her to walk around with the pin in her leg, and so she had practised walking around in such a way that nobody should notice that she had a pin in her leg and was in pain.

When she mentioned Murray this most recent time, I wanted to ask after him, or, if not exactly after him and how he was going – which didn't interest me in the least seeing that I had never met the unfortunate man in my life (although I had heard from our mother about how furious he had become since Trude's sudden and inexplicable departure, so furious that he had rung our mother several times, demanding an explanation from her, as if she had been the one to direct Trude's departure and not Trude herself) – I wanted to ask why it was that, so soon after the three-day art workshop, Trude had moved out of his place and into this pub. It was obviously a very different place to live for someone who had always, or so I remembered, lived in ordinary places like small terrace houses and flats. Even though our mother had said otherwise, I couldn't take her current residence as anything that was intended to be permanent. For one thing, it would have been expensive for what she got – and I imagined that she didn't have any cooking facilities in her room, much less her own bathroom – and for another thing, the stairs would have been a decided problem, even if, as she said, she only ever went up and down them once a day. Although she was long out of the wheelchair and away from needing to use a stick (or so I thought at the time), there still would be many months when going up and down stairs every day would be painful if not harmful.

It therefore astonished me that Trude should want to move away from the convenience of Murray's place (as described by our mother) so soon into her recovery. Trude, of course, must have been able to tell what I was thinking, because she then said not to tell her that she should move back into Murray's place. It was impossible for her to do that, she said. Now that she'd moved out, there was no turning back. I of all people shouldn't come whining from our mother to tell her what she should be doing with her life. If I thought our mother was always right, why was it that I had stayed away from Australia for so long?

Faced with such a direct question, I would like to have been direct in response. For the previous several years of my existence I had spent many long hours in journals like this one trying to understand this very question. As a child, my family had been everything to me – and of all of my family, Trude had meant the most. When I was a child I had heard that, as an adult, I would naturally want to live apart from everybody in my family, and in particular any of my older sisters. Far from suggesting future freedom or the tantalising but unimaginable pleasures of adulthood, the thought that I would naturally want to live apart from everybody in my family had oppressed me with an unbearable loneliness. I could not imagine wanting, however naturally, to live apart from everybody in my family, so I could only imagine this same thought coming out at me deviously (if naturally), waylaying me one evening when I was vulnerable and alone. It would be a thought, I used to think, which would have stalked me for weeks, always waiting for a chance to waylay me, and unless I was vulnerable and alone it wouldn't stand a chance.

Everybody in my family had been important to me, but of all of them, Trude had been the most important. We weren't particularly alike when we were very young, but I had always tried to exaggerate the features that were similar. When Trude had her hair cut, I would have my hair cut too. If she took to wearing jeans when not at school, never dresses, I too would say I never wanted to wear dresses any more, only jeans. Everything I did, when I was a child, I did in the conscious awareness of Trude and what she did. I would draw, I had realised less than a year beforehand, because Trude had always drawn. She drew girls and horses and rabbits and castles, so I drew girls and horses and rabbits and castles. She drew with her left hand, so I tried to become left-handed too. For years, beginning with the very first day I noticed that she drew with a different hand to mine, I would take my pencil in my left hand and try to draw like that. At school I was reprimanded. My writing (this was in third grade) had suddenly become illegible. I was being sloppy and careless and deliberately provocative. I was trying to become left-handed and I even succeeded.

As soon as I was able to use my left hand as easily for writing and drawing as my right, the moment I switched hands (either to the left from the right or to the right from the left), I would feel a certain process being enacted in my brain. By taking the pen or pencil in my left hand and continuing a drawing that I had begun with my right, there was a sensation as of a fogged glass being wiped clear for a moment – just a moment – before the glass would re-fog.

The result of this ambidexterity, as I told my friend Remi in France, was that I soon began to suffer from a restlessness. This hadn't been evident when I was a child. As a child, the momentarily cleared glass had only been refreshing. In classes that bored me, I would swap hands for note taking for no other reason than to stop myself from drifting off into a grey state of boredom. It was only recently that I began to realise that this ambidexterity was bound up with an appalling readiness to shirk responsibility – and not only for my actions but also for my thoughts. All my childhood and teenage years I had wanted to become Trude and as a result, I told Remi, I was able to become anything and nothing at all.

If I could have explained any of this to Trude in response to the directness of her question about my return, I might even have been able to tell her more – about how the very moment I arrived back in Australia I no longer wanted to see the sisters, the parents and relatives I'd imagined all gathered at the airport to meet me. As the plane taxied along the runway, calm now, no longer roaring, no longer straining, I began to hold onto this taxiing, this calmness, this apparent meandering of the plane, as if it had been the one desired object of more than twenty-six hours of transit in both planes and airports; as if all the planning, all the repetitions of my planning and my reasoning to other people (such as Remi), the whole edifice of the reasoning which I had developed over the months which led up to the planning and the eventual execution of my plan to return to Australia; as if all of this was now culminating in this gentle, endless taxiing of a plane whose business was only to taxi a cabinful of speechless strangers for as long as it were able. The longer the taxiing, the happier, the more bewildered I was with my situation. I had reasoned and planned for several months so that I could now be taxied in a plane that was much larger than any I had had to catch since the time I had first left Australia. The fact that I was no longer trying to imagine the faces of our sisters and our parents but was trying consciously not to think about these faces was something I was both aware of and not aware. I closed my eyes during the taxiing – for the first time in the trip no longer straining to see past the passengers sitting next to me, no longer trying to imagine the sleeping dark of the airport in Sydney (as I'd calculated it to be when I'd taken off in Paris), for the first time, as I thought, just relaxing into the journey of travelling from one hemisphere to the other. Each time the image that I had of our waiting sisters and parents came to the front of my mind, I dismissed it with the thought that I shouldn't be thinking of that image but of the last of this long journey that might be my last long journey (after all, I had planned never to live away from Australia again).

It was therefore a relief to me that neither our sisters nor our parents had actually come to the airport to meet me (in fact, they had got the time wrong, reading my morning time as an afternoon one, the mistake coming originally through our mother's interpretation of my handwriting in a fax).

I caught a taxi out to the suburb where I had last lived and then, in sudden fear of too exposed an existence – as if all the people I used to see in the streets and the bus stops around me many years previously should suddenly appear, demanding an account of all the years which had lapsed between when they had last seen me and now – I asked the taxi driver to bring me closer in to the city. I now posed as a British traveller, allowing my consonants to disappear into my mouth as I talked. I was taken to Chinatown, to a hotel owned by a friend of the taxi driver. Chinatown, I remembered saying – that'll be interesting.

I had intended to ring Trude the moment I arrived. In fact, I did ring Trude, but it was from the public telephone in the bar downstairs and it was difficult to hear what she was saying. Before I hung up, I said that I would ring her in a couple of days, when I knew what I was doing and where exactly I'd be living. I rang her again the next afternoon, at a time when I guessed Murray wouldn't yet have returned from work – nor she from her physiotherapy – but she never got back to me.

Trude raised her hand again and Charlene came over to us. She wanted to know whether the drinks were OK and, as she took our empty glasses, holding them near her waist, she offered to get us the same again.

It struck me as I watched her waddling away – the two parts of her lower back moving through the stretch top in time with her legs as if her buttocks went halfway up to her shoulder blades – that there was something comforting about someone like Charlene. Perhaps this was the main reason why Trude had decided to move here, less than half a mile, or so I'd been told, from where she had lived with Murray. It was very likely, I realised, that Murray knew that Trude was living here and had come once or twice to see whether she mightn't change her mind and try living with him again. It was also very likely that he wouldn't have thought to look in such a place and that, even if he came inside once for his own reasons, he might pretend he didn't see her, as Trude (I could imagine) would pretend she didn't see him.

With our second round of drinks, Trude began to tell me the story of the Getaway Art Workshop up north. She'd had to catch a coach there, she said. Sure, Murray could have driven her, but now that she had given in, as she put it, she wanted to get there herself and she was not up to driving as yet. The bus would be relaxing, she had told him, and besides she'd been looking forward to having all those hours to herself. Since the accident, there hadn't been a moment to herself that hadn't been centred on appointments and exercise and rest, either at clinics or at home (first at hers and then at Murray's). Since the accident, she'd traced a daily journey between bed and bathroom, between bed and bathroom and clinic, between another bed (first her own and then Murray's), another bathroom and clinic (now external to the hospital).

It drove her mad, this circumscribed existence, first in the wheelchair and then with a stick, but at all times between those same three places. Even the shops – she had grown to long to go shopping, she said, because first our mother and sisters and then, later, Murray, had seen to all the shopping that had to be done. She wished she could go on one of those whole-day shopping expeditions in a centre that she had never been to before – a prolonged expedition during which she would never once be reminded about what detrimental effect the day was having on her still far from recuperated body. All those years before the accident she had never taken advantage of this freedom to go shopping wherever and whenever it suited her. It was only after the accident, when everybody had the idea that shopping was some necessary irritation to be expunged as soon as possible, that she had developed a desire to go shopping in a place that Murray would never take her to, since he seemed to presume shopping to be as boring for her as it was for him.

The strange thing, said Trude, was that, before the accident, she had always thought of shopping as boring and tiring. She had hated shopping then, so it had been true for a while. In fact, not long after coming to consciousness in the hospital, one of her first thoughts unrelated to the pain in her body had been about how easily she would be able to wriggle out of doing all those tedious kinds of jobs that existence usually expects of people. Other people, she'd thought, would now have to go to the post office and to pay her bills. Someone else would have to do the washing-up for some time. Someone else would have to cook.

And so she'd looked forward to the journey up north. In fact, she'd found it pleasurable to be sitting in a coach that was high off the ground and aurally separate from the environment outside, this physical and aural separation being most apparent when the coach drove up the route she and Murray used to take through the North Shore suburbs to visit our parents in Pymble. She had the peculiar feeling, she said, of occupying a space a body's length above her own body as the coach took the familiar route over the bridge and up the highway towards our parents' house. But the effect of this distance, plus the strange quietness of the bus (a quietness made up of the hiss of air conditioning and the insulated turning of large engine parts beneath her) – all of this was pleasurable.

It made her think about how it might have been had she died in the accident. The bridge, the highway, the freeway would have continued to exist after she had died. So would the other people in the cars she could see from the coach window and the birds drawing lines between trees and power poles. Had she died, she might well have continued wanting to watch all these birds drawing lines from one tree to another, all these cars and coaches making journeys along the highway that would eventually pass the turn-off to our parents' house. It was soothing, watching the movement of cars and other coaches and birds and trucks. She would not have grown bored, she thought, at least not for a while. She'd heard that there were a certain number of days and weeks when the souls of newly dead people haunted all the places that were familiar to them while they had been alive. Without the bother of having bodies to lug around, these souls, or so she had heard, could move very quickly from one place to another. They didn't have to worry about being caught staring or hanging around. No one would move them on if they decided to stay in one place a little longer than was comfortable for the living.

If she had been sure she could have been able to exist in this way after death, she might even have chosen to let her body expire instead of struggling along with Murray and our parents and our sisters and doctors to keep enmeshed in the world they were part of. Our instinct was always to want to keep a hold of the material existence of our bodies, she said, because simply we hadn't allowed ourselves to think of any other kind of existence. There was no reason, for instance, if this pub continued to exist, and Charlene kept on serving and the locals kept on coming, why being dead Trude might not be able to keep being part of it for as long as she wanted, there after all being nothing to stop her.

When the coach went further up the coast and the route ceased to be familiar, she was lulled into a semi-sleep. All those houses and trees and power lines, all of them the same. All those cars, those small ones and big ones, the trucks with weather-fouled soft toys tied to their bull bars, the take-away signs by the side of the road, the petrol stations with their convenience stores behind aluminium-framed windows papered over with advertisements.

After, and even alongside, the semi-sleep came the anxiety of mistaking one of the towns the coach was passing through for the one she had to get out at – even though the coach didn't stop at any of those towns, at least not for a while. She was anxious, she said, that she might get out at one of those towns and only notice her mistake the minute that the coach pulled away from the kerb. She had never been particularly good at directions, nor remembering details like the names of places and the number of stops you had to wait before you got out. Too often on a journey, she said, the greatest pleasure was giving up all responsibility for the journey. When she used to drive, it was a different matter – although not as different as anyone might think. The car and the road would tend to drive themselves. All she had to do was keep her hands on the wheel and the journey would keep itself moving, its bitumen surface running smoothly under her. The trouble with travelling by coach or train was that all the time, against the necessity of getting off at one stop or another, there was the endless temptation of never getting off the train or coach, of taking the train or coach to the furthest destination possible, and, if the journey was an endless one, of staying endlessly on that loop of a journey.

In the end, of course, it was very easy to recognise the place where she had to get off because a couple of other people in the coach had started to stir and she heard someone mention the name of the workshop. It was funny, she said, but as soon as she heard the name of the workshop, she had drawn herself closer to the wall of the coach in her seat. It was only then that she realised what an embarrassing name for a workshop it was: the word 'Getaway' making it particularly naïve. And so, as she followed the others out of the coach, she hoped it looked, to everyone else still sitting in their seats, that she had nothing to do with such an embarrassingly naïve event as a Getaway Art Workshop.

A minibus was waiting on the other side of the road to take them to the workshop but it was only after the coach had driven off that she allowed herself to begin crossing the road behind the others. The other travellers to the workshop were a large older woman, a very young girl and a fat man. Although Trude had noticed the older woman at the bus station before they had left, and while waiting to get off the bus Trude had stood directly behind the very young-looking girl, right behind the translucent back of her head where her hair, also translucent, feathered as close as a young bird's, it wasn't until they were all pulling their bags across the road (one of those wide country roads where it didn't matter that they were jaywalking), that Trude noticed the fat man who was also with them – a fat man so fat that the skin on his face pushed out shiny and pink, as if all the room in him had already been used up but there was still more flesh to go. Just watching him cross the road with the other two, Trude said, was enough to confirm her negative feelings about the workshop. When a workshop had a fat man like this in it – a fat man who very obviously had not an artistic bone in his body – you knew that the workshop was going to be one of those failures of a workshop, where the only thing the tutors would be interested in was getting paid and eating their frequent free meals, and in the evenings, while everyone else was asleep, gossiping about what suckers all the students were: how one couldn't draw for nuts and another was so pretentious that they made everyone sick.

It wasn't hard, she'd thought then, to guess the backgrounds of the other people who had signed themselves up for the Getaway Art Workshop. The young girl, for instance, would have been fresh out of school with parents who loved her to distraction and gave her everything she wanted. They would have been parents who'd at least thought of asking her what she wanted to be or to do and then threw all their resources behind her so that she could achieve those things. Unlike herself, she imagined, this girl would have been an only child. She would have been sent to a private school – one of the smaller ones 'which cared'. She would have accompanied her parents to gallery openings and those touring exhibitions that only ever get to Canberra and never anywhere else in Australia. She would have sat with her father through contemporary operas each time her mother couldn't come, which would have been often, Trude imagined, because fathers of daughters of her sort would have contrived that their wives would have only rarely wanted to come. This girl would have got into an undergraduate course in arts and, despite all her opportunities and various abortive determinations to achieve something or other (perhaps graphic design or opera singing), she wouldn't have yet made up her mind about which direction she wanted to go in. Her parents would have then reminded her how much she used to love drawing when she was twelve and paid for her to go on this Getaway Art Workshop the moment she wondered out loud how nice it must be to have a picture in a gallery.

As for the older woman, at first Trude had assumed she was either one of the tutors of the workshop or an experienced painter on a much-needed break from the toil of deadlines. It took only a moment, though, to be aware that neither was the case. Perhaps it was the way she walked – the utter confidence and assurance of her straight-backed stride – which was more the habit, Trude observed, with people who only thought of themselves as important rather than being in any way important themselves. Trude said that at no time was she ever taken in by the way that this woman turned her head this way and that (the 'product' in her two-toned hair so thick that it shone wet), making far too audible remarks, first towards the young girl and then towards the fat man and herself, who was edging along a little after the others. The fat man at that time, she said, was wearing a pair of very dark glasses. He too carried himself erect, Trude said, but more like a child who continues to walk in such a direction as he has already been pointed in by somebody else.

It was funny, Trude said, how that woman interacted with the fat man in the beginning. To give her her due, she said (Trude was referring to the older woman), Monique would have only seen Sidney from the front, whereas Trude was coming behind him and could see the fat-fisted innocence of his hand pulling the bag. Monique saw the sunglasses whereas Trude saw the hairless bundle of his hand. The other woman saw someone who seemed unapproachable and, therefore, by a logic peculiar to women like Monique, a person whom it was always desirable to get to know. Trude, on the other hand – since she hadn't seen the sunglasses so much as the hand – took the fat man, Sidney, to be somebody unbelievably innocent and keen, one of those people who always threw themselves into an activity with the unembarrassed candour of a child.

What happened then was that during the minibus trip out to the Getaway Art Workshop, it was excruciating listening to Monique's attempts to draw out Sidney in a way that was intended to confirm that he was someone who, despite all the evidence of his hand, was supposedly an outrageous queen, a flamboyant artist of the kind who would go along to galleries and laugh at half of the exhibits; who knew certain artists and had modelled for as many. Half the time, said Trude, Sidney would just nod at one of the questions and give back a very slight smile. Half the time he would nod, the other half he would respond with one of those little phrases of encouragement which, along with the very dark sunglasses, seemed to give those same little phrases an ironic edge – which gave his 'really?' and 'I didn't know that, how interesting' a certain urbane, even cynical interpretation – especially since he had a somewhat exaggerated manner in his intonation, as of someone who was always imitating somebody else.

During the minibus journey it had been principally Monique and Sidney who did the talking. In fact, it was principally Monique who, as well as wearing so much product in her hair that it was impossible not to notice that it was there, talked so loudly – and with such an intention of being overheard – that it was difficult not to follow every word that she was saying. It was one of those occasions, said Trude, when you could easily recognise that the person who was talking to Sidney was not in fact talking to Sidney at all. Monique was talking to Sidney only in a way, Trude thought, that she might be noticed as someone who talked to an urbane and seemingly cynical artist, who might be seen therefore as someone who belonged to the world she was talking about: the world of urbane and cynical seeming artists. And so, although she was seen to be talking to Sidney, this woman with the product in her hair was in fact not talking to Sidney but talking through him to the world she thought he represented, a world that she implied was also her own. She was like someone who talked to herself when she knew other people were listening, who only talked to herself because she knew that other people were listening. She was the kind of person who said, 'Fuck, where's that damned invitation,' or 'Not here, not here, where did Mike Parr leave his address?' because she had learned over the years that it was both OK for artists to talk to themselves and OK for them to name drop when they name dropped accidentally.

Monique's conversation with herself was to be overheard, said Trude, not so much by Sidney, who would have been listening anyway, but by the young girl who was called Grace, the driver of the minibus and herself. Above all, said Trude, it was not so much Grace or herself who were to be the audience of her soliloquy, but the minibus driver who, with his faded *trompe l'oeil* T-shirt (of a cherub smashing through the edifice of the Museum of Modern Art in New York), his wizened, hairy arms and his way of jigging his left knee as he was driving, must have represented, in Monique's mind, someone who'd had something to do with the arts for a very long time. He had that look of someone who had been around for a bit and knew everything there was to know and, in the face of this knowledge, had no qualms about driving a minibus. And for all they knew at the time, he might have been the organiser of the workshop or even one of the tutors.

They were up north, said Trude, and up north there were all types. The same wizened bum in stained jeans, for example, could be a renowned theatre director or an actor hanging around the area because he had a property where he grew grass, or someone who had never had a job in his life, nor any interests other than a ready supply of beer and TAB forms. Monique would have already guessed that she and Grace were just a couple of other participants in the workshop. Only the minibus driver would have remained unknown. During the journey in the minibus, Trude said she felt nothing but impatience for this woman Monique and her soliloquies which showed off the possibility that she might (or might not) be on intimate terms with a few exclusive gallery owners in Sydney.

The workshop itself, Trude told me, was uneventful. There were twenty of them altogether. Most were from Brisbane, a few from Byron and the like, one from Armidale and the rest from Sydney. In reality, there was not much time spent analysing people's talents. It was a relief, although it might have been heartening just then, she thought, if one of the tutors had told her that hers was a talent worth pursuing. All those years of being able to draw, of delighting friends and colleagues here and there, didn't amount to much in the end because the day was divided between 'inspirational sessions' (which were discussions and all-out lectures), shorter exercises (one-minute, three-minute and five-minute sketches) and longer-running projects. Everything – the discussions, the exercises and the longer-running projects – had that arbitrary feeling of being only a product of the workshop and therefore no measure of what she might have been capable of without that extra hype. Even had she been given the space somewhere different to where she had been living – a studio already set up with drawing horses and easels and a plethora of glass jars – she began to fear that she could never have produced the material that she ended up producing during her several days at that workshop. All the same, she said, she did rediscover something in herself at the workshop, even if it was only the determination to out-do everything she saw being created around her.

The young girl Grace, as it turned out, was a very hesitant draughts-woman. She had that way of bringing everything to her drawing – a way of sitting (or standing), the beauty and concentration of her face – and it was all brought together in the immediate act of drawing, or perhaps the challenge to draw. Grace would hold the charcoal, Trude said, in an admirable and professional-looking way, as of a conductor with a baton, a singer with a gesture, but there was so much bird-like hesitation in her approach that her hand would anticipate and sketch into the air many more lines than she ever allowed herself on paper. She would seem to be working very vigorously, her hand going back and forth like a professional's, and yet if you looked over at what she was doing and watched it very closely, you would see that most of the vigorous gestures were kept for the air. More often than not, once she'd made contact with the paper, Grace would begin frowning and muttering and then immediately lift off the charcoal again. There would be five or ten minutes of this, if it was a long pose, or even seconds if it was shorter, and then 'fuck!' she'd pull out her paper from the clip, pulling and tearing it if necessary just to remove it as quickly as she could: 'Fuck this! Fuck this stupid attempt!' But all the invectives headed inwards, at herself, and so often were not even noticed.

Grace had made friends with another young woman, said Trude, who would, quite unlike her friend, work at her paper in the quietest and steadiest manner possible. Each time that Grace swore and tore away her own picture, the friend would look up and pause for a moment, not quite looking at her friend or at anything in particular, and then she would resume her own work, the details and smaller strokes being particularly absorbing of her apparent interest. She was someone, Trude noticed, who worked more with smudges and erasure than actual line. On a detail of a tablecloth corner, this friend would spend all of her time modelling the undulations of the folds with both her fingers and a small rubber, as well as a few broken sticks of carefully used charcoal. While the rest of the group would work on the whole collection of oddments that the tutor had arranged, this friend would concentrate on the comparative boredom of cloth folds. So beautiful would be these cloth folds, compared to the shadowed rendering of anything that had been placed on the table that, while the tutor often made pointed and supposedly ironical comments about how he had wasted his time scouring the outskirts of the town for objects of interest for them to draw, Trude could see that he envied the beauty of these folds and only refrained from pointing this out to the others from sheer jealousy and dislike.

There were a few older women who had come down from Brisbane and who were evident beginners, Trude said. They had apparently all worked together for the past eleven years at Australia Post. They had worked hard all their lives, putting their families before their jobs, their jobs before their interests, their supposed interests before what they really wanted. It had been decades and decades since they'd had the chance to discover what it was they might have preferred to do if life hadn't taken them over, and so when one of them (who was called Cheryl) had said she was going to spend some of her long service leave on this Getaway Art Workshop that she'd read about on a 'women and happiness' website, three of her colleagues had said they would keep her company. They would never know what they could do if they never even tried to find out, one of the women had said.

When I observed that it was interesting, considering all this, that Trude should have wanted to draw again, she shook her head and seemed to concentrate on shredding some of the raffia from the gerbera stems with a fingernail.

Nothing in the workshop, she said, made her more interested in drawing than before. It was nothing to do with the workshop per se that she had suddenly become convinced of her calling to be an artist: a real artist and no longer just an amateur pretender. All the time she had been working for those companies, doing their publicity and writing up their achievements in puke-rendering prose, she had at least enjoyed the fact that everyone knew that she could draw well and would often ask her for a little sketch for one of their PowerPoint presentations, or suggest she include a caricature of someone in one of the newsletters (which she never dared to do, but had been flattered that it had been thought of).

Since she had always done people well and, after university, had actually earned some money doing portraits of various acquaintances and friends (although she never told our mother about this), she had often dreamt that, had she been able to go part-time or become redundant, she might have found the motivation to set up her equipment to do portraits again. This in fact had not been such a remote idea. For years, during the 'nineties, she had always expected that she would be retrenched and would therefore be unemployed for a long time. Whenever her position didn't look too good in one company, however, she would usually find a position very quickly in another. All her adult life, save for a few months here and there, she had surprised herself by remaining in full employment. In the months when she didn't have a job, though, she might have tried to find her way back to portrait painting or drawing again.

From the perspective of afterwards, she told me, her time being unemployed would always look wasteful, and yet each time that it happened, she was always too anxious about finding another real job too quickly to even think that she might do otherwise and instead renew her interest in her art. Of course, she said, she hadn't had the luxury until recently of having someone else to look after her (and this she said in a certain tone as if she meant to imply that it was different for me, even though she knew full well that I had never been in that position). She'd had to earn her own money. No one else was going to make sure she didn't starve. All this was to say, she told me, that she never had to confront the reality of taking her art seriously as she had while at school and university (and immediately after university), and the workshop brought her no closer to this reality because all it did was to remind her how she used to feel when she did those Tin Sheds art workshops at university or enrolled in TAFE classes while she was still at school. In fact, it not so much reminded her of how it used to feel, but she found herself actually reliving those feelings as if nothing had happened between those years at school and university, and the time in that workshop. Yet this was not to say it was a bad experience. It was irritating and exasperating, but that was how all the workshops she had ever done in her life had been. In fact, at the end of a day at the Getaway Art Workshop, there would be such a build-up of conviction that, if only she wasn't at the workshop, she would be able to produce art that at last expressed what she had always hoped to be able to express.

She would lie awake during the evenings there just plotting how she would go about getting back into her art again and, if not quite allowing herself the stress of portrait painting, selecting a theme for a series of images that she would complete, all of which would incorporate figures in them because she had always been very good at figures. And yet this anxiety and sleeplessness did nothing else but prove how important it was for her to continue developing her talent, but only in an abstract sense. If she still thought in this way, and only in this way, she said, she would never have left Murray. Of all her situations in life, the one with Murray was the most conducive to developing her talent free from worries, because Murray already owned that house of his outright and would not have been happier, she thought, than knowing he could provide for her so that she could do what she had always dreamed of doing (a possibility, Trude realised, which must have occurred to our mother and so would have had everything to do with her recent urging to get her daughter back into her art).

What had happened in relation to her art came from a far deeper conviction than the one either Murray or our mother might have been expecting, she said. This revelation hadn't occurred at the workshop itself because, for one thing, the schedule was busy and carefully planned to focus all attention not on why they were all there trying to develop their talent, but how they could do it as quickly as they could.

Each day had started with a sort of mini-lecture and sharing session. By 'sharing', she meant that they were each encouraged to talk about their difficulties and discoveries as artists, and the tutor (sometimes more than one) would respond with stories of difficulties and discoveries of their own. There hadn't so much been any censorship of what was being said at those sharing sessions, but an unwillingness on the part of anyone there to talk about why they should even want to be spending their time developing their art. If it had been an alcoholics anonymous retreat, Trude said, or some other kind of dependency program, wouldn't they have all wanted to try to understand why it was that otherwise healthy and occasionally happy individuals would spend so much of their waking moments obsessed with pursuing their addiction? What was so different or less warped about people who had decided that they wanted to be artists and who therefore spent every moment of their lives, whether waking or sleeping, trying to further this obsession – even if, as in her case, they had spent hours and even years in remission from this obsession?

The fact that no one had wanted to talk about the origin of why they were there had not so much bothered her at the time, she said. In fact, if someone had tried to raise this issue at one of the sharing sessions, she would have been the first to be uncomfortable about this and no doubt would have concurred with the tutor if he or she had insisted inevitably that they not get caught up in this issue of 'why' but spend some time instead on the 'how'. There were some basic skills they could all learn, one of the tutors had said, and it was important to master them. It was all very well to say that you wanted to break the rules, but you first needed to know which rules you were breaking. There were certain laws about form and colour and design and, while you might have wanted to break any or all of these laws about form and colour and design some time later, first you needed to learn what they were and, more importantly, you had to master them.

When the tutor talked in this way, most of the people there had agreed very loudly. That was why they were there, one of the participants had said – this elusive 'why' – and yet the question was entirely different from the one Trude might have wanted to ask had she thought about it clearly. Instead, Trude said, she hadn't thought to question her and the others' motives for coming to the workshop, except in so far as she doubted she had made the agreeing noise along with the others – that is, agreeing with the need to master certain techniques. In fact, if she really thought about her motives for allowing herself to go along to the workshop, she could not honestly think that she had intended to go to the workshop in search of techniques. It might have been the correct motive as far as the tutors were concerned – they all very evidently thought that the participants could do with much perfecting of technique – and yet she knew how reluctant she had been to allow herself to go along with the booking Murray had made. Why was it that she had done it then? Could I even guess?

I might have wanted to say something – to hazard my own opinion based on what she had already told me – but the question she had asked me she had only asked through me. She had caught my gaze at that moment and had seemed to look into my eyes, but really (or so I was realising) all the time she was looking at and talking to me she was most particularly talking to herself.

When I was younger and still at school, I used to want to believe that she talked to me and asked me genuine questions. Sometimes, in the evenings after dinner, she would come into the room that I shared with another sister. She would come into the room and stand waiting near where I was, lying on my bed reading, I remember, or trying to do my homework, with the exercise book I was writing in undulating on the bed as I worked – she would stand in the centre of the room and wait for me to look up. She never waited long, I don't think, because I was always attuned (or so I thought) to the many and various moods of this 'creative sister' of mine. In fact, it was precisely my assuredness of being attuned to Trude (this 'creative sister') that gave me a certain status with the younger sister I had to share my room with.

To describe some of our older sisters, we two youngest sisters had variously used the words 'annoying' and 'self-righteous' and 'boring' and 'four-eyes', but Trude was the 'creative sister' – a status which had a lot of cachet for both of us at school. A teacher might remember one of our older sisters as 'bright and full of initiative', and might wonder out loud whether either of us was similar but, apart from knowing full well that the teacher was only referring to the sister that was 'annoying', we would be mortified by having it well publicised that we had a sister that was known to be such a dag. And yet the moment the same teacher wondered out loud whether either of us was 'creative like Trude', each of us would try to outdo the other in trying to prove that it was so.

Trude had drawn the cartoons in the high school newspaper. A portrait she had done of one of the teachers hung in a landing of the administrative block. Time and time again I would be asked whether Trude was my sister and time and time again I would pretend to not even be bothered to answer (although I would be trying all the more to make the doodles in my notebook as good as they could be). At home Trude would come into my room and wait for me to look up, and when I looked up she would talk to me in that casual way older children speak to younger children – as if they were doing them a favour, as if they were simply passing on information they had already told a hundred other people, and yet which I would interpret to mean that she had only told me. Trude had sought me out, I would think to myself, so she must have wanted to talk to me and to me only – even though, invariably, she would talk over any comments I made and used to turn anything I said about my own situation back around onto herself.

All these years – through high school, through my years at university and time in the public service in Canberra, through the decision to leave the country as well as all the seconds and minutes and months that I had been away from it – all these years, I now realised, I had held to the belief that she really wanted to talk to me and to me only, while all the time, I would say, I also knew that, even when she was talking to me, she could only have been talking to no one else but herself, and for this I hated her, I realised: I hated her more than I had ever hated anyone else in my life.

The moment she asked me this question, then, I also realised that I shouldn't answer it, as I had learned not to do all those years ago. I let her first ask this question of me and, obediently (while all the time conscious that I hated her), I said nothing at all.

The only reason she had gone along with Murray and his stupid advance booking of the workshop, Trude said, was that she saw it as a test. She knew that if she could stand being in such a situation, where she would either be taken for a complete and gormless beginner or, with all her experience and skill acknowledged, shown up all the same for a failure who had wasted everybody's time for so many years (not the least being her own) – if she could stand such a situation, she told me, she knew she would be able to progress; that she would be able to call herself (if only in her own company) an artist.

When she talked of herself as an artist, even in this very removed, very ironical way, Trude seemed not to be able to help the way her face slightly altered as she pronounced the word. There was some apology, some caution, in the way she pronounced it, and at the same time her face, which until that moment had been animated in the unselfconscious act of talking – at the same moment her face had grown very still. It was if the word 'artist' had been excised from the rest of what she was saying and been held a little forward of all the other words. It was also as if she had said out loud the kind of sexual word that she might have used countless times with her friends and her lovers and, only as she was saying it, felt the incongruity of saying such a word in front of such an over- (and indeed under-) familiar person as her sister.

In the end, of course, such a question as whether or not to call herself an artist was neither here nor there, she said. During the workshop, it was never really a question, particularly as it was assumed that they were already artists: all of them, from the very rawest and least talented, to the most proficient among them. It was taken for granted, she said, that they – all of them – were artists, and yet at the same time they were always made aware of the fact that the tutors were somehow more real as artists than those who had simply paid to be there at the workshop. Those who were paid, then, were the real artists, and those who did the paying had only, it seemed, the provisional right to call themselves artists.

All the time during the workshop, the tutors had praised their commitment to their work as artists, which from context, said Trude, was very evidently only the fact of their having paid for and then come to this workshop away from all the pressures of their ordinary lives. At the workshop, surrounded by the inspiration of nature, they at last had the opportunity to explore the creativity they all had there within them, the creativity being something they all supposedly had but was usually neither visible nor accessible, she said, except through a process of releasing. They had to access their creativity, they were told, through the discipline of becoming sensitive to their visual environment. Only through drawing or painting, one tutor had told them, could they release this creativity, and more specifically through the discipline of doing a series of one-minute sketches, followed by two- and then five- and then ten-minute sketches (they needn't be confined to traditional media, although the whole point of the exercise was to free up the arm, which would then tap into the wells of creativity they all had inside them).

When the tutors talked to them about the wells of creativity inside them, Trude had thought about some kind of secret hole in the red of her flesh. She then thought of a precious and miraculously undamaged organ she might have had, like the bile duct, or the adrenal gland – some hidden and hitherto unknown fount of particular substances. It was like the appendix, she said, as if the appendix, rather than being just a throwback from the stone age, from an era of eating grasses and other indigestible foods, was in fact a gland that secreted a pure and unfamiliar fluid into the bloodstream the moment it was released.

She knew, however, that she wasn't going to have the revelation of her own very real calling to be an artist from being among people who were always drawing and talking about drawing in the way that, in hospitals, there were always people experiencing nausea and vomiting and therefore also wanting to talk about their nausea and vomiting.

If she had hoped, even subconsciously, that somebody would notice her capacity to draw – in the way at her various workplaces, as it had been at school, she had always been known as the person who could draw – she pretty soon forgot about this as the workshop got going.

Their first day wasn't much of a day, since they had all spent most of it travelling. Since it was an out of the way venue – the out of the way nature of the venue being particularly useful, they were told, for releasing their creativity – most of them, whether they had come from Sydney or Brisbane, had had to travel quite a distance.

Perhaps, Trude wondered, the whole point of such a Getaway Art Workshop was that the participants first needed to travel a great distance from where they usually lived, as if removing themselves from their usual environments were essential to the releasing process. There was practically nobody from any rural areas. There was one person from Armidale and a couple from Byron Bay, but apart from that, the rest of them were from the major cities nearby. In fact, nobody was anything but a town- or city-dwelling person. Perhaps there had been another Getaway Art Workshop, she'd begun to wonder, for rural people who needed to go to a town or city to release their creativity. Rather than being surrounded by the inspiration of nature, they would have been surrounded by the inspiration of human environments: the idea of human environments being very much in vogue, she'd noticed, among the tutors and some of her fellow participants. A still life was a still life but it was also an example of a piece of human environment. There were ways to talk about your experience which made it instantly recognisable as belonging to the art world.

Part of the point of workshops, she'd begun to think, was to pick up the kind of language you needed to put your artwork in context. Without the right language, you would never be able to interest a gallery in an exhibition, however small, of your works. While you were supposed to release your creativity, you were also supposed to develop your work in such a way as it could be given a context. If you liked drawing people, it wasn't enough to say, simply, that you liked drawing people. Nobody would be interested in an exhibition of someone who only liked drawing people. You needed to use the language you were given – that, in a sense, you had paid to acquire, perhaps through several workshops along similar lines – to form a context for your drawings, in the way that an egg needed a nest. You can't leave an egg on a table, it rolls off, Trude said. This was how one seemingly eccentric tutor had described the use of verbal context. If you put an uncooked egg on a table it will roll in one direction or another and, if your table is slightly sloping, it will roll off the table entirely. So too, the tutor had said, an exhibition of drawings can come to grief without an appropriate context.

It was only after the workshop had finished and they were already on their way home, Trude said, that it became at all possible for the real issues to be made apparent to her, and that she might begin to know her own heart away from the well-meaning pressures of Murray and our mother.

Having just told me this, Trude seemed to look past me. She was looking at a spot that might have been a couple of centimetres out and several metres back from the lower right side of my face. After a short while, she then turned all the way round and looked as far behind her as she could without moving too much of her torso. While her head was turned in this way, I could see that her hair, which had once been long and thick (many years ago, I had to admit), looked now somewhat thinner as well as shorter, and there was a patch behind her ear where the hair seemed very sparse (a patch which might have continued around the back of her skull but of which I could only see one edge). The scantness of her hair made me think of babies and old people and made me realise that, however much I had admired and looked up to this sister when I was young – a looking up to which had been precipitately shattered, as I'd once put it in a journal, when she failed to be the artist that I expected and had instead gone to university, done a social work degree and later taken a public relations job in an engineering firm – my admiration of this sister had always been accompanied by a certain readiness to observe in her all the physical and emotional deficiencies I might have otherwise only expected to observe in somebody I didn't like.

Even as a child, I began to see, I'd had this perspective. Parallel with admiring and looking up to my sister, I had been glad, for example, to notice that all the time she could draw so well her fingers had been ugly – much uglier than mine. Her fingers had been long, I used to grant, but they had also been paler and bulbous at their ends – as bulbous as a bunch of shallots, I used to think. This bulbous effect had been created partly by the way the ends of her fingers tipped outwards from their topmost joint, and partly by the fact that she always chewed her fingernails, not only to the quick but beyond the quick. It was as if, while she was chewing at her fingernails, she could never be satisfied by chewing off the loose parts of her fingernails – the parts that weren't connected to her body – but was driven to chew further, so that there might not be even the very beginning parts of a fingernail that was not connected to her; that by shredding at what was left of the edge of her fingernails she might prevent there being any fingernail that could grow separate from her (this shredding of the fingernail only adding to the image of the white, bloodless roots of distorted shallots).

It was no different now, I was noticing: the way that I was looking at her. Although her fingers were not the same – the fingernails were shortish but

I could see they were no longer being bitten or shredded past the quick –
I found myself still looking every now and then at her fingers, as if soon I
would find the evidence of what could only have been an act of perverse
destruction whose resulting shallot ugliness had always given me a thrill of
satisfaction. Although her fingernails were not how they had been when
I was a child, I noticed that the scantness of the hair behind her ears had
given me the same thrill of satisfaction. I knew this was not the same as the
thrill of satisfaction I would have got from the sight of her shredded shallot fingernails (since the scantness of the hair made me think of a passive
rather than an active perversity of destruction: something which she not
only couldn't help but which had been foisted on her against her will).

I tried dismissing this thrill of satisfaction by thinking of the pain Trude
would have had to endure during and since the accident – what had to have
been excruciating (and hence unimaginable) amounts of pain and stress.
The loss of hair, I tried to tell myself, would have been caused by this pain
and stress, as well as all the long hours she would have lain in a bed without
being able to move herself. She would have lain like that since the accident all day and all night for many days and weeks and unendurable hours.
There had been considerable damage to her pelvis and to one of her legs,
I remembered hearing, and so it would have been dangerous to turn her.
She would have to have lain still. Although I knew nothing about convalescence and the healing of bones, I tried to cover over my satisfaction at
this sign of her physical weakness by trying to estimate how many days it
would have been that she hadn't been able to move. Our mother had once
told me how long it had been but I had already forgotten it.

At that point I had sent Trude a card, but only to salve my conscience
that I hadn't yet made arrangements to visit her in Australia, in her new
man's house. It would not have been appropriate to visit Trude at her new
man's house, I had told myself. She was only then settling in and it would
not have been very pleasant to have sisters coming over to check out her
new man on the pretext of visiting her to see how she was going with her
recovery. Such had been my reasoning, I remembered, when I had sent her

that funny card about the chicken in the fridge.

When Trude turned back round to face me, she looked once again past me towards that spot in the distance but didn't say anything, only waited. I knew that at this point I should have asked her what had happened on the way back from the workshop, only it seemed redundant to ask her such a question – and worse, it would have appeared stupid.

So often, I realised (all too conscious of my previous thoughts), I either said something to Trude because it seemed to be what was required by the situation, or I stopped myself from saying something that might have been appropriate to say at that moment, but each time I was only aware of one thing – how stupid I sounded or was going to sound. This was not just a fear of sounding stupid. I actually very often sounded stupid, or at least that is the impression I had always got from Trude – her way of looking at me after I said something that either challenged what she was saying or was an attempt to start a new topic (over which she would start talking again with an irritation that was only very barely suppressed). All it ever took to silence me was this particular look from Trude, which I can best describe as a slow looking round (or across) at me, the slowness of this look being the best indicator of her opinion of what I had just started or was going to say.

All the same, I reminded myself that I was also the only one, or so I was often told by our mother, who some of our sisters would ever talk to whenever there was a crisis of some sort and they refused to talk to our mother (or I should say, refused to be subjected to her inevitable tirade). I was the sister several of my sisters used to tell things to, perhaps because I was someone who, because of my crippling fear of giving offence, was usually unable to interrupt (unless to give further impetus to their story), even when I felt bored out of my skull, or when there were more pressing reasons, as when I had a particular train to catch or lecture to go to.

Throughout my life, both overseas and in Australia, I had often been told how good I was at listening. I was also presumed, I soon discovered, to have taken in much more than I had actually taken in. After telling me at great length, for example, about her difficulties with her Cambridge supervisor, a friend in London had once rung me up in the dead of night at least a year or two later just to tell me a further instalment, as she put it, in the farce of her doctorate. At first I hadn't realised what she was talking about. As it was, it had taken me some minutes to place her voice. The only people who rang me at inopportune times back then were usually people from Australia. It had taken me some time to realise that the 'Jackie' who was talking to me wasn't the 'Jackie' who had been a friend of Trude's for some years before they had parted ways in their adulthood. Since she evidently assumed I remembered everything she had told me the last time I had been in London, this Jackie, whom I eventually began to place, started her description of what had happened by referring to that paper she had given in February. I was so disconcerted by this reference to 'that paper', it became all the more difficult to follow this further instalment, but since I was not required, or so it seemed, to give a full account of what I understood, the conversation ended up concluding very well, with Jackie telling me how much she valued my support and had taken to heart what I told her the previous time we had spoken.

While still looking past me, Trude took hold of a stick that she had laid across the seats of a couple of chairs at the next table and pulled herself up on it. She suggested that we go upstairs to her room. At this I demurred. It was a long way up all those stairs, I said, and didn't she usually only go up them and down them once in a day? Trude turned her slow eyes towards me (that look I was dreading). She didn't exactly want everybody to hear what she was telling me, she said (and saying this with the implication that she knew I wouldn't have thought of its dangers: since I was someone, as she used to tell me often, who could be extraordinarily vague).

At this point, I might have smiled to myself. I knew (I was thinking) that she was surely exaggerating. Who on earth apart from her family, I was thinking, would find the story of her deciding to become a serious artist and then leaving her new boyfriend as anything but an uninteresting story, it neither concerning them nor anybody that they knew? If Murray had been there, the situation would have been different. Even Charlene might have been curious, if only to learn how long, perhaps, this client of hers intended staying at the pub.

This way of taking herself very seriously I have both admired and despised (more than despised, I was now realising). All through my childhood I longed to grow up so that, along with breasts, I might gain a sense of importance in the way that I could see that Trude had. Only through growing into my own importance, I thought then, could I have any basis on which to dare to take myself seriously.

Trude got herself up on her feet and I was relieved to see that she didn't walk like an old woman (as if the scant hair behind her ears had made me think that she would). In fact, she seemed to be quick on her feet. Perhaps, I told myself, she was suddenly feeling a whole lot better.

This last thought of mine, despite the recent realisation of a long-developing hatred for my sister, gave me cause to feel satisfied. In all my years of being a listener for my sisters and some friends I had, parallel to a frustration that I was usually unable to control the listening role I'd been put in (or so I have written in other journals), I was also easily convinced of the virtues of being a good listener, as well as confident of its renowned good effects. No doubt, or so I reasoned at the time, by being able to tell me so much and feeling ready to tell me still more – even the crux of the matter – Trude had found a new energy in herself thanks to my presence; an energy (perhaps) she didn't know she possessed until after she had already told me all this I have related, all this that was only the lead-up to the main things she wanted to say.

II

I was shocked when I saw Trude's room in the hotel, not because it was messy (I would have understood a messy room), but because her room, conversely, was tidy, as well as crammed with the meticulous order of clear plastic labelled boxes of papers and what was probably clothing. It was a tidy, box-crammed room, the plastic boxes arranged on a wooden shelving system that was so new that the first thing I noticed was the smell of pine.

Trude must have guessed my surprise because she gave me another of those slow sidelong glances. She then placed the wallet folder, the book and the still wrapped gerberas on something that might have been a converted wooden crate that had been set up next to her bed. Just because you don't know how to be tidy, she might have said to me, you seem to think that nobody else knows how.

And yet it wasn't so much that it looked tidy, but that it looked semi-permanent. Trude had evidently gone somewhere to buy all those lidded plastic boxes and all that shelving and had someone put the whole thing together for her. Most of the boxes, I realised, would have been inaccessible to her and therefore useless for day-to-day use – at least until Trude had more strength and mobility. When you can barely support your own weight, I was thinking, you can't exactly pull out one of these clear plastic boxes from a higher shelf at the same time as you are standing. The boxes weren't as big as some plastic boxes are, and yet, all the same, they wouldn't have weighed nothing. More than anything else those clear plastic boxes with their lids, and the carefully arranged shelving, suggested to me that our mother would have gained nothing by sending me along to Trude to help her see sense and move back in with Murray.

Not long after we both settled ourselves on her bed, which was the only place we could sit in her room – she sitting up on her bed with her legs lying horizontal and I on one side of the bed, turned round so that I could face her – Trude told me that this was all that she had brought with her to Murray's place and hence from there to the pub. When he'd suggested she move into his place not long after she had come out of hospital, whatever else people had thought of the decision, she had only ever thought of the move as a temporary arrangement. It was convenient to be so close to a hospital, even if it wasn't the hospital she'd been involved with before, and since his place was a single-storey house, unlike the place she'd been renting, that was also an advantage. When she moved, she organised that all her furniture would go into storage. This meant that she could give up her lease, the storage costing nothing in comparison. Murray and the removalist company had packed up her place for her. All the furniture and household items such as crockery and buckets went into storage, she said: the television, her mirrors, even her easel and her oil paints, they all went into storage. She liked this forced reduction of her way of living. One day she would get out her oils, but she wasn't ready yet.

Living with Murray had been convenient, she said. When he helped her move, he hadn't yet found out about her past interest in art. She could have told him, but she didn't want to tell him about it just then. At the beginning there had been no point in telling him about her interest in art because, as well as being irritated by our mother's suggestions, she also didn't imagine she would stay with Murray for long. There were many things about Murray she hadn't thought she could stand for the long term. Even at the beginning, when everybody talked about how miraculous her recovery had been and how romantic that she should have developed a relationship with the very man who had saved her life – even then she'd had no intention of staying long with Murray. In fact, it was because of the miracle of her recovery and the romance of developing a relationship with the man who had purportedly saved her life that she'd expected that their relationship had no future to speak of. The more people talked about the miracle and the romance, the more she felt sickened by being at the centre of this miracle and romance.

It was not that Murray had actually started all this rumour, she said. It was nothing to do with him. He was embarrassed when people talked of their romance, as embarrassed as she was. If somebody came to his house when she was there and they referred to either the miracle of her recovery or the part of the romance in this miracle of her recovery – the part of romance that was as good as any film story – even if they never actually mentioned any of these words per se but only referred to their existence in the way that they sat on Murray's sofas or offered to carry the tray of coffee cups – if either of these words seeped somehow into Murray's house, she would notice how he would mostly look at the floor and withdraw from the conversation. He had a way, said Trude, of mostly looking at the floor and saying the least that it was possible to say. When he looked at the floor in this way, people would seem to respect the privacy of their relationship. This meant that, having let slip the idea that they had been thinking either of the miracle of the recovery or the role of romance in this miracle, the visitor would usually be too polite to suggest anything more in what they said or did. Instead they would change the topic, said Trude, and begin to talk very volubly about their own travel plans or the state of their renovations. But all the time they would be talking about travel or renovations they would be smiling, as if either their travel plans or their renovations had somehow a secret link to the romance or the miracle of Trude and her film-story recovery.

What she realised now was that the situation of the miracle of her recovery and the part of the romance in this miracle of her recovery allowed her friends to give full vent to their discussions of their travel plans and their renovations. Previously, when she was neither in a relationship nor living in a house that was owned not rented, she thought it must have been difficult for her friends to talk about such things in her company. How could they talk of travelling with their husbands or boyfriends without all the time being conscious that their friend Trude didn't have either a husband or boyfriend to travel with? When they used to talk about such things in the past, they had always been careful to make light of their boyfriends and husbands as well as their travel plans because they were always conscious, Trude thought, of trying to avoid giving offence.

One of her friends had a husband who snored. Even at the early age of forty his doctor had already warned him that his snoring, coupled with his recent weight gain, was dangerous for his health. His doctor had advised him to get a special device that closed over his mouth and nose while he slept, forcing air into his lungs. This device he had taken to with the same enthusiasm, her friend had told her, as he had recently taken to those devices that removed air from bottles of wine, and so wherever they planned to go on their travels, they had to make sure that the accommodation was suitable (as far as power points went) for the accommodation of this air-forcing device, which meant that they could no longer just travel wherever they wanted to but were compelled, in advance, to check out the accommodation for its suitability and then book this accommodation straight away so that they didn't miss out. This friend, said Trude, seemed to be very happy to talk on and on about her husband's problem and the special needs of their travel arrangements now that she perceived her friend Trude to also have special needs after both her miraculous recovery and the new situation of her romance. This friend would lean forward as she talked about her husband in a way she had never leaned forward whenever she had mentioned him before the romance. This friend, however, was always sensitive enough not to talk in this way about her husband when Murray was actually there in the room with them. Instead the friend would make sure that, after Murray had sat for a time staring down at the floor, she would ask in an over bright voice for a glass of water with ice or something equally fiddly, knowing full well that only Murray and not Trude would have to leave the room to get it and also knowing, or seeming to know, that Murray would guess by this request that he should stay in the kitchen (which was a little way down the hall) a bit longer than it would actually take him to empty some ice cubes into a glass of water.

While Trude was telling me all this, there was a glaze over her eyes from the brightness of the outside coming through the balcony doors opposite her. She had positioned the bed so that her feet, and therefore the whole orientation of her body when she was lying on her bed, looked outwards at the sky over the tops of the buildings across the road from the pub. Although her eyes would have adjusted, I thought, to the brightness of the sky (which that day was as smooth and pitiful as those pieces of starling eggshells you find everywhere in the city these days), from where I was sitting, the reflection of the squares of sky on her corneas gave an unpleasant impression – as if, as well as having to recover from injuries to her pelvis and leg, she had the problem of an eye condition that she might have picked up since she had left the hospital: a condition she might have picked up either from Murray's place or the pub.

I amused myself with thinking that this was why our mother hadn't wanted to come here again and why she had sent me in her place. Our mother has a horror of places like pubs because they remind her of her own upbringing, she used to say, in Croydon. Her parents hadn't known better, supposedly, but there was nothing worse than the beery smell of glazed pub tiles when they had been wiped over very cursorily with soapy water. The smell of soapy water always reminded her of the beery (and often urine-sweet) smell of the tiles in the pubs her father, and later her brother, used to go to in Croydon and Burwood and in other suburbs further away. There would be years of rancid beer, concentrated urine and even more disgusting substances in the grouting between the tiles, which couldn't be removed with just a dose of soapy water. Even today, our mother thought, the best and most modern disinfectants wouldn't be able to remove the tuberculosis-infected spittle that would have been aimed at the tiles near the entrance of such places. It was only a matter of time, she thought, before all the diseases she had seen in her childhood re-emerged from the foul porous places in which they had been hiding for years. It was the reason she had insisted that she and our father move from the family home in Croydon to a newly built house on an escarpment near the bush in Pymble after their wedding. The most important thing you had to do in life, she used to tell me, is to face up to reality.

It could only have been our mother's fear of pubs which had prompted her to send me in her place as listener and sympathiser, as she would unfailingly try to flatter me into believing myself to be. All my life, I had either been flattered or bullied into acting as the right-hand woman of our mother, whose role I only managed on occasion to wriggle out of by running away. Whatever I did – whether succumbing or running away – I knew our mother had succeeded in removing something of *my* self so that she could put the stronger will of *her* self in my place. Even my resistance to her work of replacing *my* self with *her* self only succeeded more effectively in allowing *my* self to be replaced with *her* self. I had gone overseas by *my* self and stayed there, living there for many years, and yet, just by removing *my* self there (removing my self to the other end of the world from my mother) – particularly when I was living in Paris – I was living the kind of daughterly existence that it suits a mother like ours to claim for *her* self, and hers became the existence of a mother who has a daughter living overseas and, particularly, in Paris. Even coming to this pub, I reflected, I had acted as much out of resistance to our mother's dislike of pubs as I had complied with the pressure she invariably brought to bear on me. There has been no way I have ever been able to effect an escape from this role of both being the right-hand woman of our mother and having *my* self replaced by *her* self. It is a role, I have always thought, that I must have been born into. Although I am one of several sisters – and perhaps all of us have been asked to do this at one time or other in our early lives – I am the only one, it seems, who has in fact fulfilled this role for our mother (and *our* selves). The more I have resisted it, the more I have fulfilled this role without even knowing that I have been doing it (or so I began to realise then).

In Trude's new accommodation, with her both closer to me and more removed from everybody else in our family than she had been for over a decade, I would have liked to be able to discuss this very problem that has always dogged my existence. I would have liked to ask how it had been for her all those years living in the same city as our parents and several of our older sisters – I would have liked to ask how it was that she could avoid being directed to do things in the way that I had always been directed to do things (not only by threats but also by flattery and tears). I would have liked to ask how it was that Trude had been able to do not one thing that our mother had ever approved of and, when at last (and tardily) one of her relationships with someone was given the maternal approval, and she had got back into her art as apparently directed, Trude had moved out so suddenly and to such a place that our mother's relief and elation had turned into despair.

I wanted to put it to Trude, then, that her reason for moving away from Murray had been solely because our mother had willed it, her approval being death to any one substantial and important thing that we might have wanted to do for our selves. I wanted to say this and might even have done so – because after talking about Murray and his house Trude had grown silent for a short time – but it didn't seem the right time, I thought then, as I watched her, for interrupting her silence.

All our lives, I thought, our silences have been interrupted, and if mine have been more effectively interrupted, it was no reason, I knew, to interrupt someone else's. Many have been the times when I have been directed and coerced and flattered into interrupting one of my several sisters' silences. It would be suggested that I ring, that I write – that I both ring and write. Or I could call in on one of my sisters, because I should know how they always liked being called in on.

In getting out of the country I had been able to strike myself off from this list of daughters who could call in on other daughters. In France I used to wonder that perhaps one of my other sisters had been made to take my place in my absence. It had been a long time. It had been nearly ten years, I used to think, so it was very likely that in my absence another daughter of our mother had been given the primary role of interrupting one of the other daughters' silences. And yet I was still asked to ring and to write – primarily to write. When, while overseas, I would say how little time I had for such things, our mother would tell me that an email didn't take a minute, that some people just sent any old rubbish. They spent their whole lives sending out rubbish via email. Our mother didn't use email, but she had heard about email from her friends. Some people, she said, just sent a single line, she had heard. A single line could be enough.

I looked over at Trude. Her mouth was moving slightly, in the way that people replay in their minds a conversation that has just happened or a conversation that they dread. She was busy with her thoughts. I had no right to interrupt, I told myself again, however much I disliked her. If only my thoughts had never been interrupted, I might never have gone to Paris or London. I might instead have gone to Bolivia, I thought, or another country our mother has never shown the least inclination to visit or have a daughter installed in. I might have become a meteorologist, I thought – she would never have thought of that. There was no end to the possibilities of my self, I was thinking, if I had only been able to give full rein to my self.

It was awkward and painful sitting on the bed in this way. My legs were turned in one direction and my torso in another. Also, the expression on Trude's face as she was thinking disturbed me for some reason, not least because of the unpleasant way her eyes had been glazed by the glare outside.

I stood up and stretched, turning my body in the opposite direction to the way it had been sitting, and walked over to the balcony doors. There was very little I could see over the railing, only telegraph wires and a mottling of masonry and roofing. There was the sky of course. I was sick of the sky. This was what I thought as I looked out the windows of Trude's balcony doors: I am sick of the sky, I am sick of the sky.

In truth, though, I have always loved the sky, particularly as it was that day, a blue, nearly clear sky (there were one or two wisps of cloud). Broken and as blue as an eggshell, I thought, those starling eggshells that make me think of imported pests such as cockroaches and mice. All day, and particularly in the late afternoon, this kind of wide blue and often fragmented sky that you only ever see in Australia arouses strong feelings in me. There is both space – an infinity of space – in such a sky, and a brutal absence of it. Sometimes, I was thinking as I looked out over the roofs and through the wires, the sky is nothing more than pieces of coloured paper that have been stuck between objects, between those roofs and wires, over the spaces between objects, so that we might not see beyond them. It is as if the sky had been expressly invented to block what lies behind it. The sky might have been invented by our mother, I could have said to Trude.

When I had been still living overseas I had avoided most kinds of contact with my sisters and with Trude. Every year I would send them one of those Internet birthday cards. For bigger birthdays I even used to send them a present. My other sisters would usually thank me and return my email with a colourless short message. Trude would never reply and I wouldn't be sure whether she had got the email or present at all. There were many sisters in our family and I could imagine that Trude would be busy because if everyone sent something at the same time, that would mean a lot of writing emails and letters. I could understand that she didn't have time. In fact, I was also to some extent aware that my clock-perfect email cards or presents were generated out of a bitterness I still felt about the neglect I had suffered as one of the younger sisters in a numerous family.

Before I moved overseas, I had lived a few streets away from Trude and yet I never used to visit her. I never seemed to think of it. I used to see her hurrying, sometimes, on her way to the station, but the most I would do was to raise a hand in greeting, or call out a hello. During that time I used to remind myself that I should one day call in on her, if only because she was the sister I most admired and had most in common with, or so I thought then. My ongoing resistance to this idea I interpreted as laziness and, while no doubt it was always laziness, it was also nothing more than a resistance I could never understand.

For some people, I think, moving to Europe or America has been a way of enabling themselves to be closer to what they believe is the centre of things. In Australia, or so this reasoning goes, we are so far away from the centre of things that the most we can do is to imitate those people in the centre. All of our artists and writers and models and film stars may look very much like the artists and writers and models and films stars of the centre, but this is only, or so the reasoning goes, because they have become adept at imitating what they cannot possess by right of birth. The fact that many move themselves to either America or Europe and insert themselves faultlessly into the films and beauty pageants there – so faultlessly, it seems, that the local audiences of those countries will be spooked when they discover that the only actor who sounds as if she comes from Los Angeles in a television show is the one actor who is not only not from Los Angeles, but isn't even American (because Australian) – this fact only makes it clearer that imitation is our greatest skill.

I can understand this reasoning, and to a certain extent I am an imitator myself, but for me moving to Europe was not a way to move myself closer to a centre but to remove myself from a centre (which was my family) so that I could exist in the strangeness of a periphery. To an English-speaker like myself, living in France was an acceptable periphery. I had at least learned some of the language before my departure and the thought of losing myself in this other language – of losing myself among people who were (as I thought then) completely other to me – this thought was an erotic thought. The first days, the first weeks, were charged with this eroticism. At the end of the first year I was happy that I was celebrating my new otherness alone in a flat whose only view was of a courtyard full of damp cardboard boxes. I was happy that, after a few years, no one could tell that I was an English speaker. There was something strange about my accent, I would be told – the strangeness of an adult who speaks French with too clear and artificial an enunciation – but this I couldn't hear in what I was saying.

I revelled in this strangeness. This had been what I had wanted, or so I used to think. All my life, I would tell my friend Remi, I have wanted nothing more than this half-light, this oddness. When I left for France, I might have been thinking of the Paris of Proust, of Balzac, of Lautrec – and yet all the time I knew that I would never find those parts of it that they evoke in their work, that the most I could hope for was the 'network of dark streets' that some of them refer to only in passing: a 'network of dark streets' which I then wished to be endless and endlessly mine.

And yet it was in one such street that I experienced the first of my amnesias, as I would tell Remi, when I would be walking: walking and concentrating only on the unevenness of the pavement and the texture of filth pushing out of the fissures, walking and suddenly becoming overwhelmed by the mechanics of my walking, the meaninglessness of my walking, the complete and utter stupefaction in the face of the immediate reason for my walking. At such a time I couldn't bring to mind why it was I was walking in that particular direction and then, suddenly alarmed at not being able to remember such a thing (despite a lifetime of very occasional and similar minor lapses of memory), I would try calling to mind something a little more distant, such as what I had done the previous day or the previous Sunday – even my name, I would challenge myself with my name – and frightened by the absence of thought, I would be able to recall nothing other than the anxiety of my attempt to remember, the unevenness of the paving and the pullulating filth growing large in my mind. The only way to get past such an attack of amnesia, I would tell Remi, would be to force myself to continue walking in the same direction I had been walking in until that moment. It would be the very last thing I would feel like doing – as if by continuing to walk I would end up walking over the edge of my memory, never to return – and yet somehow, there would always be something that would distract me from my frightening lacuna – something as small as the descent of a sparrow onto a bin, or the fleeting expression on someone else's face – and I would continue with my walking, no longer concerned that I didn't know where I was going, the reason having emerged like a stick floating silently and gently to the surface again.

These amnesias kept on happening to me, as I once tried explaining to Remi, either because there had been a sudden and definite onset of degeneration in my brain (a possibility which I couldn't overlook) or because, over the years, I had grown so disconnected from everything that had once defined me as a child, and later as an adolescent. When you are an adult, it takes a little time to realise that you need to come full circle. Early in adulthood there is always the possibility that you will become something very different from how you have always known yourself to be. Everybody affirms this, from your teachers to your parents, your older siblings and your friends. You put away childish things, you tell yourself, and become the adult you cannot even quite imagine. It is only later, much later, as I told Remi, that those small adjustments of early adulthood that we once made for ourselves seem laughable and in themselves childish.

In my early twenties I used to wear eye make-up. Every day I would put on foundation and eyeliner and stiffen my eyelashes with mascara. When I was younger I was not worried that the colour was already beginning to drain out of my face but would instead be concerned only to make my face look paler and my eyes considerably larger and more soulful than they were – all this so that I could become the person, or so I thought, that I wanted to be.

Remi would laugh when I told him about the eye make-up. Remi was my neighbour in Paris. He was at least fifteen years older than I was and would wear such rumpled-looking clothing that it would seem as if he had only dressed to match the rumpled-looking lugubriousness of his face. Whenever I went over to his place, he would put on some bitter coffee and bend over to rustle around in his cupboards, looking for something that wasn't out of date. He seemed never to have anything to eat that wasn't out of date when I called in. He used to be a writer, he had once told me, but now he did copy for an online real estate company.

At one stage early on, I thought he had been interested in me, but that had been my error (or so I realised afterwards, when I found out he was still seeing his ex) and had come from reading too much into his patience and attention to whatever I used to tell him. About a year before I left, he had suggested that I move in with him, but I knew he was only trying to be kind, to help me save the money I was spending on extra rent after my Italian flatmates left. He had seemed hurt that I thanked him for offering and didn't contact me for a while (making sure he wasn't home during the evenings) – not until he knocked on my door to tell me he had a couple of free tickets to a one-woman show he'd picked up from a friend in Toulouse.

Remi could be like that – these inexplicable silences – but otherwise he was an extremely patient person, the most patient in the world. I never once saw him irritated with anything more than the uselessness of his larder. It was while I was talking to Remi in his flat not long after Trude's accident that I suddenly realised that if I was going to go to Australia to visit her, I shouldn't ever come back to France. For the past several months and years, I had been talking on about this problem, my inner disconnection, as I called it, and yet it wasn't until I was talking to Remi about Trude's accident – and the short visit that I was planning – that I realised that I should stay in Australia and never leave it again. Going back to Australia would be a gathering in of myself, I tried explaining to him, in contrast to the constant dissipation of the last several years: the constant dissipation as evidenced by the episodes of amnesia and other strange attacks of not knowing where I was or why I had just walked into a room with a pencil and a stapler in my hands (and was very likely caused by a certain two-faced quality I have always had in relation to my family and anybody very close to me – a two-facedness that I now wanted to overcome).

I was very taken with this idea of gathering myself in. It was a new idea, I thought. It had taken me a lifetime to understand such a fundamental idea as this one to the health of my brain, even the health of my soul. Life would be different when I got back to Australia, I then told Remi several times, because I had at last worked out how I needed to live.

It was disappointing but Remi, quite uncharacteristically, had taken issue with the idea that I had at last worked out how I needed to live. He said that I had to be careful with the idea that life would be different when I got back to Australia. Sure (he had said), it would be different in the sense that the place, the people, the smells would be different, but taken as an essential, he said (giving emphasis to this idea of the 'essential'), the experience of life would not be different at all. Life was never different in any essential way, he said, and we always over-estimated the value of the experiences we had left in the past. Distance gave a false connection to things; time made a soap opera (*un mélo*) out of what could only turn out, on closer inspection, to be a series of very ordinary occurrences and misunderstandings.

I had got annoyed when Remi had taken issue with what I was saying when he implied that I was trying to turn my past into *un mélo*. All I was trying to do was to gather myself in. It was a difficult decision I had to make, perhaps the most difficult decision I'd ever had to make in my life. He had no right to make fun of my decision to gather myself in. He himself had hardly led a life free from wrong moves and false interpretations. He had been a writer, as he had put it, but had never been happy with the work he had done; he had perhaps wasted years and years of his life along this false path of a 'writer', when he might have lived more comfortably in a less illusion-prone profession. Even his work for the online real estate company: he couldn't pretend that he loved what he was doing (in fact, I knew that he was embarrassed by it and often pretended he was an ordinary newspaper back room journalist or a real estate agent instead). All I had was my intuition and my intuition was telling me that moving back to Australia was the right thing to do. The very least he could do for me, I said, was to respect what I was saying. If at last I had worked out how I needed to live, he needed to respect that and not try to undermine me. It had taken years – a lifetime – to understand such a fundamental idea, and I didn't want to waste any more of the years I had left.

In France, in Paris, I had thought all this with great intensity – the intensity making each of my moves towards emptying my flat and giving notice at work and buying my ticket have the slow luminosity of great moments in film – and yet, I reflected near the windows of Trude's balcony doors, I was also aware that all through my life there have been many times when I have been convinced that I had only just worked out how I needed to live. At the point of realising that I have at last discovered how I needed to live, I have always thought of the various factors which have led up to the moment of realising this: these factors taking shape in my brain in a series of stills. Just trying to recall those moments when I have enjoyed the intensity of these thoughts is enough to remind me of certain of these stills. There is a particular still, for example, of myself in a plane slowly landing in Singapore airport. In this still, it is night and the night spreads wide beyond the bubble-clear windows of the plane. The plane is tilting and so it seems that the runway and the city, lit up by countless points of light arranged in lines and building shapes, are tilting instead of the plane. All there exists of this first country beyond Australia that I have seen is a tilting of light points that stretch outwards into infinity. This still – an image of otherness, as of something being dipped in a large cold pool – this still, I now realised, is usually the first of a series of like images which I invariably bring out for any realisation that I have only now worked out how I needed to live.

It was at this moment that Trude turned on a light. The light was only one of those small desktop study lamps that she had placed on the box beside her bed. The room didn't really need a light – it was still early enough in the day – but the light somehow made it easier to stop thinking about myself. Perhaps it helped Trude to come out of her reverie too because I saw that she had swung her legs off the bed as if she wanted to get up again. We were to go out onto the balcony. It was better, she said, to move around and not stay still, particularly in bed. If she just stayed still in bed all day – and she might have organised it, Charlene was very helpful, the best nurse there was – if she just stayed in bed all day, she would never get better and never be able to become the artist she knew she was meant to be. This last sentence she let fall very easily and casually. It was as if she was unaware of the particular words she had chosen, or as if their meaning was less significant than the words themselves pretended to be. For some reason her casual way of saying such a sentence roused such bitterness in me that I was thinking again how much I disliked her. Perhaps it wouldn't have been so bad, I thought, had there been any sign of her art work in this meticulously arranged room. If she had already started work on becoming an artist, the fact that she had hidden all traces of it made me think that either she didn't trust me or that she thought my attentions to it would be not worth the trouble of showing it. I tried imagining an easel set up in the room. I imagined a canvas on it, and a stack of canvases against the wall. Then again, it was likely that it was only her way of talking about such a thing that stirred up my bitterness – that way of talking that assumes the person being spoken to is all ears about the special status of the speaker, that way of speaking that assumes that nothing on earth is more important that this special status which, ironically, is best talked about as if it were nothing.

She now talked of her situation with a candour that was disdainful. It would be good neither for her recovery nor her art to stay in one place every moment of the day because when she was alone and in her bed she tended just to replay old conversations. It was as if the bed was the one place where everything came to rest and became moribund, with all the dross of her previous life holding fast to her body. Ideally, she thought, existence shouldn't be this contingent. In an ideal world, it shouldn't matter where she was.

If I had been writing to Trude in an email, it would have been easier to respond to what she had just said. 'So you're not completely happy yet,' I might have written. It would have cost me nothing to write something like that, whereas to say such a thing would have felt too provocative. On the other hand, I thought, saying something like 'so you're not completely happy yet' could not be seen as provocative at all, since it would only have been mirroring back, as I have heard it said in teaching circles, what Trude had already indicated to me, and yet I knew that I wasn't up to facing the defensive tirade that would inevitably follow. This I could only have done while writing, because when I write I am not quite the person that I feel myself to be at other times in my life.

Trude opened the balcony doors with difficulty. They mustn't have been opened for some time. The moment the doors opened the sound of cars rushed in on us. Trude moved crab-wise around one side of a large plastic table that took up most of the room on her balcony. She hadn't brought anything with her apart from her stick.

Outside, among the layered noises of brakes and birds and distant trains, Trude's face seemed to light up with renewed energy. Hers was a small face, a little smaller – I'd always thought – than mine. All our early lives, despite not looking like each other at all, people used to think we were twins, partly because of my efforts to look like her and partly because Trude was petite and I was tall for my age. As babies we didn't look anything alike and even ten years ago we had nothing visually in common that might have marked each of us out as the other's sister, but in the years we had been apart we had grown more alike and, among the noises and the weak reflected light that had come this far into the deep shadow of the balcony, it was possible to observe the way we picked up little gestures and expressions from the other – as when the raising of her eyebrows after she looked towards me now found an automatic response in the raising of mine.

I had to try to imagine what it was like, she said, the day she returned from the Getaway Art Workshop, the day she should have returned. There had been a storm the evening before. The roads near the camp were too muddy for the minibus. After those who had driven had already left, the organisers were going to take the others back to town in a couple of the tutors' four-wheel drives, but it was only then that they realised that the back seats had been removed. Then someone had the idea of going back down the river in the boat that belonged to the local. This local came up the river every day because he was building himself a house on the hill behind the workshop. All they needed to do was to wait for him to show up. The problem was that he ran late that day, probably because of the storm the night before. They waited around all morning and were already preparing to squat illegally in the back of the four-wheel drives, when the local turned up and agreed to ferry them back down the river.

It was great on the river, said Trude. It should have been part of the Getaway Art Workshop from the beginning – the addition of the words 'only accessible by boat' would have packed out the workshop with even more of those people who were itching to make a vast difference to their lives. Everybody had a hankering to be somewhere remote and inaccessible. For many people, she thought, creativity and inaccessibility were basically the same thing.

When the boat pulled alongside the little wharf, the sun was already beginning to set. Someone gave a cheer and one or two people got out their digital cameras and took scenes of everyone gesturing and posturing in front of the water.

As it turned out, Trude said, they were too late for the coach back to Sydney. Those going back to Brisbane were all right. They still had a couple of hours.

When they got into town, they all chipped in for a bottle of whisky for the local and his boat. They went into the nearest pub with a bottle shop and picked out the most expensive whisky they could see. Everyone was on a high from the success of their Getaway Art Workshop, or else someone sensible would have suggested just an ordinary slab of beer. It was ridiculous, Trude said, but the Getaway Art Workshop had obviously worked.

Something had happened to all of them, she'd realised. If they talked to one another, the idea of being creative was implicit in what they said and how they responded to things. There was a largeness in their gestures, a loudness to their speech. It was as if somebody was following them about and filming what they were doing and would later piece together this episode into the larger, greater drama of their lives.

Once they discovered that it was too late to catch the coach back to Sydney, the woman called Monique suggested all the Sydney people go back to the pub where they had bought the whisky. She had always wanted to stay in one of those old country pubs, she said, with their you beaut, old world atmosphere. Since her divorce she was making herself do things that she had always wanted to do but hadn't let herself while she was married. It was the only way that you got over those barriers that you erected on all sides around you; the only way you got past the stultifying habits that grew on you like mould. The fat man, Sidney, hadn't liked this idea much, said Trude, but the rest of them travelling to Sydney had talked him down. They were obviously still high on the aftermath of the workshop. Perhaps there was a motel around the place, he had suggested. He started to plead the difficulties that Trude was obviously having just walking around, and the others had just stared at her, which was highly embarrassing. It was far worse to have her concerns championed by such a man as Sidney than to have to endure a lot of stairs. To cover over her embarrassment, she said, she had voted for the pub. It was also already in front of them. It was the easiest thing. They needn't even bother trying anywhere else.

There was another reason that Monique had wanted to stay in the pub, said Trude. This was connected to the man she had met in the bottle shop when the rest of them sent her up to the front to buy the whisky on her credit card. She'd spent some time chatting to the man at the till, Trude remembered. They could all hear her laughing and carrying on as she handed over her card. Monique had this screech when she laughed, said Trude, and they had all heard it in the bottle shop.

Monique went into the bottle shop to find the man she had been talking to before. She'd said she was going to sweeten him up for a deal. She wanted everyone else to come too just to meet this guy and see what she meant, so they all got ready to follow on after her.

There was a stupid moment then, said Trude, which was not worth recalling in itself except for how it made her realise something important that she should have realised long, long beforehand. No one else would have noticed that this thing had even happened. Monique had walked on ahead, she said, but the rest of them were on par with each other. Sidney, the fat man, was a little slow but that was more due to his reluctance to go back to that pub. There were only two other people coming with them: the pale girl called Grace and her new friend from the workshop called Jay who Trude had assumed had made her own way by car to the camp, but obviously hadn't. Grace and Jay had got together during the camp, she'd realised. She hadn't been surprised.

The bottle shop, said Trude, was separated from the rest of the pub by a sliding glass door. At one time, the door must have slid across just the refrigerated section of the bottles, because it had the look, she thought, of doing more than simply separating one section of the pub from the rest of it. Perhaps it was a way to discourage those in the pub from going into the bottle shop and buying their own bottle of something that they could scoff from under the tables. The usual entrance to the bottle shop was from a door in the side of the pub, but they had all entered the pub through the main bar that day and followed the signs through. Both times they had gone into the bottle shop they had had to slide open the glass door and then slide it back shut because there was a sign on the door that said 'please shut door' in large black letters on a gold piece of card. The first time they had gone into the bottle shop there hadn't been any problems with the door, but the second time, after Monique and then the couple and Sidney had gone through, one of them (it might have been Sidney or Jay) had given the door such a shove that it began to slide closed again of its own accord, effectively threatening to shut Trude out from the bottle shop and the discussion about the accommodation.

Several things, she said, had passed through her mind as she watched the door sliding shut in front of her. Being not so mobile since the accident, she said, her first inclination had been to panic, for some reason, that she wouldn't be able to walk quickly enough to get through the door before it closed. It was interesting, she said, that for no logical reason, her first inclination had been to panic. It was as if getting into that bottle shop was the most important thing in her life – if only just past that door – and her inability to walk quickly meant that she was unable to do anything about a disastrous consequence that would bear down on her unless she could get through the door before it slid shut in front of her face.

She had tended to think of herself as no longer being superstitious, or to put it another way, there had been a time when she had been susceptible to not being able to see the world as any different from the carefully worked significance of books and films. In a film, for instance, a door that is about to slide shut of its own accord might represent a moment of urgent choice, an opportunity that is about to vanish, or the inexorable workings of a world beyond control. As an adolescent, she said, this was how she had looked out at her life. And yet as a child the superstition had been simpler. When she was a child, she would set herself a task: say being able to take only two strides between a couple of trees, or to jump from a branch without falling forwards onto her knees. If I can jump and land on my feet without falling, she would tell herself, this boy or that boy will fall in love with me and marry me. If I can hold my breath the whole way up this flight of stairs, I'll become a famous artist and not die until I'm old. As a child it had been simple. The rewards or otherwise of a sliding door were unequivocal.

And then, as a suggestible adolescent, this had grown more complex and became more similar to the way she began to understand films. For a filmgoer, the meaning of a sliding door might not be known until after the event. A filmgoer sees a door sliding in a movie and sees the heroine react to it in one way or another. The heroine must move forwards in the film but the filmgoer doesn't need to do anything but sit back and wait for the sliding door to make sense later. It might not happen for several scenes, said

Trude, or perhaps not until the end. A good film, though, will not have a sliding door for nothing. Chekhov once said that if you have a gun in a play it needs to go off before the play finishes. When a child sees a gun, she expects it to go off straight away, but a filmgoer knows to sit tight and wait for the gun to intrude during the climax of the film.

She was no longer a child and no longer an adolescent, and yet the door sliding shut fanned a panic in her. She saw it again through the eyes of a filmgoer, and so she could only see it as representing a disaster or at best, an urgent and life-changing choice. The panic overtook her. It was stupid, she said, and it was only a measure of her suggestibility after the workshop that she should have let herself be panicked by a door that was sliding shut. She'd thought until that moment that, unlike the others, she hadn't been affected by all the talk of creativity and images at the workshop, but the door had shown her otherwise. Before the workshop, she thought, the door would just have been a door and not a symbol of an impending disaster or an urgent and life-changing choice. She might have just waited for the door to close in front of her and then, when it closed, simply opened it again straight away and followed the others into the bottle shop where they were organising the accommodation. The door would have been only a door, and even if it had been heavy, somebody might have come and helped her to open it, either one of her colleagues from the workshop or somebody from the bar.

As it was, though, she was so unnerved by this incident with the door that she didn't even try to open it after it had slid shut in front of her. For a moment, she just stood in front of the door and pretended to be interested in reading the instructions on the glass. Wherever she looked in the pub, there were written instructions of some sort. The door had to be closed, it was written; no alcohol bought in the bottle shop could be consumed in the bar. The door to the bottle shop was locked at nine in the evenings. All purchases of liquor had to be accompanied by proof of age if required. Warning: 24-hour surveillance in operation.

As a result, of course, she had no say in the arrangements. The accommodation section of the hotel had been closed for some months, but Monique and the others struck a deal with the man in the bottle shop who, as it turned out, was the brother of the owner and manager of the hotel. But it didn't matter, Trude said, that she didn't have a say. Although she still felt herself shaken by the incident of the door, and felt for no reason that something significant and even terrible was going to happen, she also at the same time was quite happy that the decision about the accommodation had been taken out of her hands.

She was all the time imagining an impending disaster or urgent and life-changing choice, and yet alongside this she was happy with the arrangements because the night in the pub was going to be cheap – and it was all decided by other people, not herself. If they had stayed at the motel or at one of the other pubs in the town, it would have been far more expensive, Monique had said. They were all going to have to semi-camp, but the sound of it was exciting. They were all artists, so they shouldn't mind a little renovation going on around them: a bit of bare render, some old peeling paint. In fact, it was romantic, Monique said, romantic in an arty sense, to be staying in a place that was in the middle of being transformed. Even Sidney, who had initially been so unhappy about going back to that pub, seemed to smile when Monique mentioned the word 'romantic' as they all followed the brother of the owner and manager back into the bar and out through a door to a corridor behind.

From the outside and from the front, said Trude, the hotel had looked more like one of those buildings that had spent twenty years of its existence being the only bank in town. It didn't look like the front of a pub. As such, said Trude, it was interesting that Monique had picked it. Even when they had first got to town, Monique had gone on and on about the old pubs that you can find in the country. Out of all the pubs she might have chosen for them to go looking for the whisky, the pub they had found seemed the least like one of the old pubs she had been describing (at least from the outside). The curved pale brick ribs on the façade were very 'thirties. It might have even been the façade of one of those old cinemas where the grey slate steps to the single glass door had been worn thin on one side from those elderly cinema-goers who preferred to use the railing. Old credit card stickers on the glass hinted that the building had probably once housed a restaurant, and yet the moment they went in through the doors they were sure it was a pub. It had that smell of a good pub, where the beer and nicotine have sunk deep into the woodwork. It was surprising, Trude said, but it was definitely a pub.

When they met the owner and manager of the pub in the corridor behind the bar, they were so taken aback by his appearance that nobody, not even Monique, might have guessed he was the owner. The man from the bottle shop – ostensibly the brother of this owner and manager – was so unlike the man they met in the corridor that it wasn't possible to believe they were brothers. The brother in the bottle shop seemed so savvy, as Monique had said. The first time in the bottle shop, he had talked about the pub and the renovations as if he had just rolled up there from Paddington in Sydney. The fact that the outside and the inside of the pub hadn't matched had seemed obvious and entirely in keeping with the very savvy style of the brother in the bottle shop. He had also talked about the pub with Monique using the word 'we' as he described what was being done to it. When he had mentioned the words 'Dave' and 'we', she had assumed at first that he was talking about his partner, and not just a business partner.

Monique might have wanted to stay in an old-fashioned pub, said Trude, but it was obvious to everyone later that she only wanted to investigate the accommodation there because it was not at all like the other pubs in town. She might have talked about it as if it were an old-fashioned pub, but the most old-fashioned aspect of the place was the smell of the woodwork in the bar. In truth, said my sister, the place was very much a hotchpotch. Perhaps it had been bought up in the 'sixties and only then turned into a pub. It didn't take many years of marinating to turn a previously odourless place into a rancid pub. The smell of the place was comforting, she said. She herself had always liked the smell of pubs.

Trude now leaned forward a little as she continued her story. Although she still didn't catch my eyes (which were now turned down towards the dull white of the plastic table between us) I sensed an unusual intimacy in her tone. We have never been an intimate family. During emotional movies on television, should any of us have let a tear descend from our eyes, the rest of us would have jeered. In a family like ours, what intimacy we have experienced has too often been a disguise for attempts on the part of our parents to crawl into us, to manipulate our thoughts. Instinctively, then, as Trude leaned forward, I leaned backwards as far as I could. She might have raised her eyes to meet mine but I was looking away, over the shopfronts opposite us, my eyes pursuing that infinitely distant point that I knew to exist beyond the particles in the air that had turned the sky blue.

It was interesting but when we were all young, Trude now told me, I mightn't remember this – in fact, I probably hadn't been born – our mother often had to drive down to Lidcombe to check up on Uncle Cec. Our mother used to be regularly rung on weekends by one of her much older sisters. Uncle Cec, Trude reminded me, was the only brother of our mother, and while his sisters all got married and moved away from the inner western suburbs of Sydney, Cec had moved further west and, after a stint working on the Snowy Mountains scheme and supposedly living in sin with the sister of one of his Polish workmates (unless it was the Polish man himself), had stayed single all his life. He could be a bitter old bastard, said Trude. Seems he'd lost a lot of money on horses some time back and so the sisters tried to look after him, which meant calling him up in the evenings to ask him to family events which he never failed to turn down for one reason or another. Sometimes it would be days and weeks before they could get hold of him because the telephone would ring and no one would answer. The sisters suspected he just pulled out the cord from the socket, but they could never be sure.

Our mother didn't want to get too involved in the whole thing because his way of life depressed her, Trude said. She'd told her other sisters that it was all that she could do to look after her own numerous daughters. It wasn't easy, our mother used to tell her older sisters, when you had a husband who didn't pull his weight, neither at home nor at the office. Her husband worked hard enough at the office – harder than most ordinary husbands and fathers, our mother used to say – but he was never strategic about how hard he worked. He worked in a small family business, for a man who used to be a great friend of our grandfather, which meant that it was impossible for our father ever to do anything more than work his hardest for the man, while expecting little or no reward (since our grandfather was long dead). Our mother would be furious with our father for being seemingly blind to his own needs and yet infinitely accommodating to the needs of a man whose claims to friendship with his father were dubious to say the least.

Our father's father had been killed very suddenly and this supposed friend of our father's hadn't even come to the funeral. He had been called away to Adelaide, but he hadn't actually left at the time our grandfather had died. He could very easily have put off the visit to Adelaide which, according to our mother, was only one of those routine and very useless excursions that he went on regularly during the time that our father worked for him. There was never any evidence that those visits to Adelaide were anything but the slightest pretext for visiting a winery he was known to have bought into in the early 'sixties. And what was more, our mother used to say, she was certain that this friend of our grandfather had someone else there in Adelaide: a young floozy, no doubt, because otherwise why would he have needed or wanted to go there so often? As well as the winery he had a factory in Adelaide, which was always the pretext for the visits, but the needs of the factory were so minor that he was able to get away with our father fielding any technical enquiries over the phone. It was very likely that when our father's boss went down to Adelaide he didn't even bother to call in at the factory he was supposedly checking up on, and his wife would never have dared to question him on the matter. Our mother knew our father's boss and his wife, and so she was sure he knew that his wife wasn't the kind of person who would ever dare to bring up the very dubious question of the boss's regular visits to Adelaide.

And yet when our father's boss suddenly died, it was his wife who very rapidly and efficiently took over the business, and who had no compunction in asking the most personal questions of 'your father' (as our mother used to call him to our face, said Trude). She would want to know in meticulous detail the hours he kept at the office and those that were necessary on occasion for the much larger factory they oversaw in Silverwater. Silverwater had no wineries and no floozies, and our father's trips out to Silverwater were always done at our own expense, our father apparently thinking it mean-minded even to keep receipts for his very minor fuel expenses for such an excursion.

It was ridiculous what our father used to put up with, our mother would say. None of her sisters had such a husband to deal with. They all complained about their circumstances, but they really could not even begin to comprehend how it was living day-to-day and week-to-week in a family like ours. Our father, said Trude, always earned the very minimum that he possibly could earn – even less, according to our mother, since she had discovered that new graduates in engineering without the Masters degree that our father had spent years of his life slaving at his own expense to get – even new graduates in their early twenties earned more money than our father earned. Our father had a large family to support, but this had never melted the heart of either his boss or, later, the wife of his boss (who became the new boss). They must have seen how we all had to live, our mother used to say, not one of us being able either to learn the piano or go to a private school.

More than anything else, she regretted not being able to send any of us to a reputable private school for girls. This was the reason we had turned out the way we had. If our father had had an ounce of self-respect, we needn't have lived in this way, but as it was, one day crawled into the next, one day becoming another (without moment, without advantage). This was why, she used to tell Trude, our only hope was either to marry somebody rich or get a good profession. It was the classic Jane Austen scenario, said Trude, only at least in those days we had the option of a career.

And yet none of us had wanted to comply with these wishes. We were all to be either doctors or lawyers of various sorts and yet we all dropped, in year eleven, those very subjects that were best calculated to get us the highest marks possible. We were fools, said our mother. We were worse than our father. One day we would understand, she used to say, why it was she was so anxious on our behalf. Even if we didn't actually want to become doctors ourselves, we might at the very least marry one of the nice young men that we would meet during our studies and at the social events associated with our studies. We were far worse than our father, she said, because at least we had a mother who actually cared enough about our future not to get us tied up with a boss who was not at all interested in our welfare. Only a mother, she would say, cared enough about her children to give them the very best in life. No one else – and she would say she had learned this from bitter experience – no one else cared as much for their children as a mother did.

And yet none of this was ever understood by her sisters, which was why they would ring her up every now and then, dumping the responsibility of looking for Uncle Cec entirely upon her. She was a mother, and yet it would never have entered the heads of her sisters that she had children to be responsible for – her sisters being so wealthy that they had arranged their lives so as to be the least bothered by responsibility for their own children (one of her sisters had even got her children to be weekly boarders in a school less than five miles from their home). Her sisters, our mother would say, were so little concerned for the actual circumstances of our family, that they would expect her to dump everything and go off in the early evening looking for Uncle Cec. Although any normal husband and father would have already returned from the office by the time she had to leave to look for Uncle Cec, our father was not such a father. She couldn't even have left us at his office to be babysat because, for one thing, he would usually not be there but would still be out at the factory in Silverwater or would have left for Blacktown, for one of the suppliers' warehouses. And for another thing, such would be the circumstances of the office that it would not be possible to leave children there anyway. Dangerous chemicals used to be left routinely around the place, in easy reach of young children or toddlers. Every time she went to our father's office, there would be trays of ammonia as well as other noxious chemicals lying uncovered in the corridor or on the fire stairs outside the rooms. These chemicals would always be either on the floor or on one of the low filing cabinets. They were in easy reach of any toddler, let alone a young child, and – what was more, and even more serious, she used to say – our father seemed to have no understanding, no understanding at all about how dangerous these chemicals were to anybody, let alone children. She could not trust his judgement. He simply had no idea.

This was why, our mother used to tell Trude, she used to have to drag all of us over to Lidcombe to look for Uncle Cec in the pubs, going from one pub to another until she found the poor sodden fool. She would drive either over the bridge or via Parramatta, with us shoved hurriedly in the back, usually already bathed and in our pyjamas, said Trude. There we were, still smelling of soap and fresh, stiff towels – all four or so of us crammed in the back of the old Peugeot – that old 1959 Peugeot whose peculiar engine sound had been rubbed into our memories from very earliest times. We wouldn't be allowed to get out at the various pubs that our mother used to drag us to. Instead we were instructed to lock the doors and keep the windows wound up and not let any man entice us out of the car. Once, said Trude, a huge blowfly was caught in the cabin of the car with us when our mother – who must have succeeded in finding Uncle Cec – was taking a very great amount of time inside a particular pub. One sister had squashed that fly against the window and the fly had exploded into a writhing white mess of tiny maggots that slipped down the glass in a run of mucous. It was disgusting, said Trude, but we didn't know how to clean it up, and yet we were frightened of the maggots and frightened of the pub. Our mother had told us so many horror stories about pubs that we didn't dare go out of the car and into the pub to try looking for her.

Even today, said Trude, the sound of blowflies made her think of that time. She had wanted to go out to get our mother, she said, but she was also too scared of what she might find in the pub even to open the door. When our mother eventually turned up, with her hands on either side of Uncle Cec's shoulders so that she could steer him towards the car, she was so disgusted, or so our mother had said, by the state of her brother as well as the state of the bar he had chosen to waste his money in, that she didn't even notice the maggots, which had already – by that time – dropped off the glass and the window sill onto the seat and our clothes. We were crying and wriggling and screaming, but she didn't notice there were maggots in our clothes or in the car. She just thought we'd been fighting amongst ourselves as usual. As she tried to steer Uncle Cec into the front passenger seat of the car (holding the front door open with her body and pushing half from behind him and half from one side) she could see us crying and pushing each other in the other direction from the maggoty window. Since she thought we were fighting amongst ourselves, even fighting amongst ourselves to be as far from the side of the car that our vomit-smelling, beer-smelling, piss-smelling Uncle had got in from (the vomit and the beer and the piss being as sweet as roses then and yet also as frustrating in the way it obscured the main concern: the whereabouts of the maggots), the moment she had pushed him sufficiently in from the passenger side of the car, our mother had leaned in over behind him and hit out at us with her open hand.

There were four or so of us there, said Trude, and so she hit out at us four or so times. Each of us might have been hit once or one might have been hit more than once, she said, but the effect was the same. The tears running down our faces were swallowed, but each of us felt she had swallowed a maggot. Although our mother often used to hit us when she was desperate, as she would say, there was something shocking about this particular strike of hers and what happened afterwards, Trude said. While our mother often caught the back of our legs with a wooden spoon or pushed us suddenly from behind, so suddenly that our heads jerked forwards, this time was different. Not because of the pain of it (it was no more or less painful than any other such occasion) but because of the way it had very quickly ceased to be just a physical pain.

When one of us had started crying and attempting to regurgitate the slippery salt of a maggot, our mother had grown furious, more furious than Trude had ever witnessed in her life. Our mother must have thought that we were reacting to the smell of Uncle Cec, Trude said, because she began to cry and say that she had never known such rude and ungrateful children, or such a stupid and desperate situation. She was desperate, she said, and no one was listening. We had no idea how desperate she was. She had then looked around at us with a terrible bitterness, a look which communicated nothing but the bitterness of her hatred (of us, of Uncle Cec, of our father, of our life) and of her wish to exterminate everything and all of us (if only, said that look: if only she could find a way).

From that moment in her life, Trude said, she knew she would never be able to trust our mother. Often later, as a child she would think about the terrible bitterness in that look she had given us after the hit with the maggots, and about what our mother would do to us if only she could find a way. It was a harsh conclusion to come to, she realised now, but probably only realistic. Children could be very realistic creatures. When she used to think about this look of bitterness – this wish to exterminate everything and all of us – Trude said that she began to think very differently about everything our mother had ever said to us. If you didn't trust your mother, she said, you soon realised you could never trust anything she said or urged you to do.

It was perhaps as a consequence, said Trude, that she soon thought of the trips out to the pubs on the other side of Sydney as exciting events. At no other time in her early life did she go on such adventures. When the phone calls came, she and her sisters were pushed into the bath. All of us would usually bathe together – sometimes in one batch, sometimes in two – and when our mother had been called out to Lidcombe, there was urgency in this demand. Our mother would be irritable and rough, sometimes scratching us with her nails as she helped us to undress, but the urgency was contagious. We would know we were going out with her, going out in the car. There was nothing we liked better than these excursions in the car – not to the shops or the school, but somewhere far away and unknown. It was very likely that she herself was the only one who loved these excursions, Trude said.

When we drove up the highway or out on Epping Road, we would pass car yards and other pubs and the poor houses of people who had to live in terrible conditions, as our mother used to tell us. She used to point out such places: old terraces and squashed semis, which had been forced between shopfronts and were bare to the heavy traffic on the road we were driving on. This is why, she used to say after she had pointed out one such derelict or obviously under-loved house between yet another row of dusty milk bars and takeaway chicken shops – this is why, she would say, I want you to get a profession. No one is going to look after you; you either have to get a good job or marry someone with a good job. If you don't, she would say, you'll live in horrible and lonely houses like these.

Whenever she looked out at the places our mother would point out and invariably disparage, Trude would still feel a little of the revulsion that our mother had wanted us to feel. Those houses certainly looked unloved and dusty and grimy with pollution. They also looked airless and friendless and hopeless and sad. And yet, along with this revulsion, there was always fascination. It would be dark in those houses, she would think, the passing traffic would drone all night, and yet she could see herself in such a place, lying on a shabby bed, on unwashed sheets, and listening to the traffic as it droned along the road outside (the play of headlights through the shabby curtains as comforting as television). She would be alone in such a place, she said. There would only be that droning and that shabbiness, that flickering of headlights through the holes in the curtains and the rings on the railings. It was voluptuous, this image of herself in the friendless place, the horrible and lonely house.

This had been with her ever since, she said – all her life there had been the comfort of this possibility. The pubs too, she said – all those pubs she used to see, those whiffs of beer and urine and sweat she would get when the car door opened and our uncle was pushed in – the pubs too began to look comforting, because they were horrible in the same way as those houses on the main roads were. This had always been the last thing – the last thing that could ever be taken away from her. She knew that if the rest of her life fell apart, she said, there would always be the comfort of such houses, the houses even more than the pubs. It had only been since the accident that she realised this – in fact sometime later than the accident (although related in its way to the accident). It all hinged, she said, on this time after the workshop: not the workshop itself but the time after the workshop. It is usually not until afterwards that we ever realise the significance of anything, she told me. We are always living our lives in this afterwards mode.

It was only afterwards, too, Trude said, that she realised what it was about the pub owner and manager – that man called Dave they all met in the corridor behind the main bar of that pub – it was only afterwards that she realised what it was about that man which, if not exactly comforting, she said, was fascinating all the same. I had to understand, she said, how very unlike his brother he was. While the brother in the bottle shop had been large and savvy, the brother in the corridor was the complete opposite in every respect. Dave was a little man – or if not exactly little (he would have been taller than she was, she guessed) – but compact and bristling in the way that compact, hairy men with thin exposed arms and legs can bristle. He was wearing a torn polo shirt and had thin, hairy legs under a creasing of shorts. All in all, Trude said, he looked like a high school sports teacher – exactly like a high school sports teacher – perhaps even the very same sports teacher she and all the rest of us had shared for over a decade at the local high school. She did not think of this at the time. At the time her only thoughts were how unlike he was to his brother and how unlike an owner and manager of a pub he looked. She didn't think of the sports teacher connection until much afterwards, when she had already got back to Sydney, but when she thought of it later, it explained something about her feeling that he didn't at all look like the owner of a pub nor the brother of someone as voluble and large and evidently caring of his appearance as the man in the bottle shop had been: the man who had appealed to Monique by seeming to be so likeable and savvy.

And yet, without knowing it, Trude said, she thought she had begun to be connected through this man, this Dave, to the self who was her high school self. Already, through his influence, she had begun thinking of herself as part of a group, in the way she had been part of a class at high school, and yet resisting this idea of being part of a class or a group (a classic adolescent resistance).

This man Dave, Trude said, evidently saw all of the travellers as the same, as part of the same kind of group: those people, as he said, who go on those arty camps up the river. He was always seeing people who arrived in the town go on some sort of arty-farty camp up at the place his friend Joel had sold years ago. No one should ever have touched that dump up the river that Joel had fixed up, but Joel was a cunning bastard and got some arty-farty people interested in taking it over. Joel himself had bought it off some hippies in the 'seventies who had started building the place with termite-ridden timber. They were such idiots, they didn't even realise that the timber they had brought up the river was already being eaten by termites. They probably thought the dust that came off the timber as they drilled into it was authentic dust, arty-farty dust, and the idiots never thought to ask someone who might have told them straight that they had been diddled with the timber. Joel had a job of it, he said, ridding the place of the termites. Stupid time-wasters the lot of them, both the hippies and the new lot. Joel might have done himself an agreeable shack up the river. The locals liked fishing up the river and so it might have come in handy for some of the mates Joel had, but he'd been hoodwinked by these arty-farty time-wasters and so had had to pass it on. You only had to look at the idiots who bussed in from the capital cities just to sit out by the side of that weed-infested and mosquito-ridden river to waste their time making pictures of their own bloody navels.

When his brother (from the bottle shop) said some of these time-wasters were right in front of him and had been very interested in everything he was telling them, Dave had looked at him with that look that sports teachers give other teachers who interrupt a good rant. It didn't matter, Trude thought, whether Dave realised that we had all come from the art camp or were just some tourists passing through. It didn't matter in the least for the effect of his rant. Some teachers, she thought, just wanted an audience to rant to. It didn't matter whether they were talking to the right people or about the right people to the wrong people, as with those teachers who would keep everyone in after school because someone had written something rude on a door. The fact that it might have been another class or even a teacher who had written this rude thing on the door was neither here nor there to the teacher who just felt like a rant and so wanted to rant at a group of kids he would have to keep back after school so he could enjoy the fact that he had imprisoned somebody, just for the enjoyment of imprisoning somebody for a crime whose details he had already forgotten.

As a result, Trude said, she found herself being lumped in with the others – not only the other people who were with her (Monique, Sidney, Grace and Jay) but all the other arty-farty people Dave had seen arriving in the town and going out to the art centre in the minibus that met them – all those people who, as he implied, were both admirable (in contrast to his bristling, narrow manner) and ridiculous in their naivety, in their stupidity, at mistaking the termite dust in a plank of wood for the authenticity of a natural piece of wood from a forest.

It was Dave, Trude said, who told them that his brother William would cook them dinner if they wanted it, and that he didn't mind where they stayed upstairs. It wasn't finished, he said; they were mad to want to stay there. It could only have been William who had talked them into staying in unfit accommodation, so the more fool they if they wanted to do it. He could provide sheets if he could find them, and blankets (probably in one of the cupboards at the top of the stairs). He wanted cash for the accommodation. There was an autobank down the road, next to the chemist. His accommodation not being finished, he didn't want any fool paperwork, there being enough to do what with the renovations and keeping tabs on Mad Dog and Elaine. Some people, he said, would have given up the business years ago. Some people weren't such a fool's fool as would try to make a fair kind of living in a fool's kind of place.

But for the distraction of Dave's ranting, said Trude, she might have realised that it would have been a good idea to ring Murray to tell him she wasn't coming in on the coach that night. She hadn't brought a mobile with her. This had been intentional. Murray had wanted her to bring her mobile phone but it had been the last thing she had wanted to take on a Getaway Art Workshop. She had already been told there was no reception at the camp. There had been a landline at the camp, and so Murray would have been able to ring her there if he'd wanted to. Either of them could have rung the other. Of course she'd had no intention, she said, of ringing him from the workshop. Once she'd agreed to go there (and at Murray's expense) the small attraction of going had been to get away from Murray and his house and the world that moved around him and the self that had grown comfortable existing in his world.

It wasn't that she was sick of him, she said. It was not a matter of being sick of Murray – in fact she had grown to love him, to really love him – but always being around him was just too much. It needn't have been Murray. It could have been anybody: Viggo Mortensen, Brad Pitt, David Beckham, and she would still have felt the same. It was comforting being around somebody all the time and being immersed in their world – and especially somebody you knew had been destined for you by the peculiarities of fate – and yet she really missed that other comfort of hers, which had been her own company and being at the farthest remove from anybody who knew her. She had given in to his idea of exploring what she had always wanted, of releasing the potential she had always had for her art, and this was mainly because she had wanted to see what would happen – whether she would be able to continue with her interest in drawing despite all the adversities that such a workshop would bring up – but partly (and she realised this more now) because it seemed to make Murray happy to think he was providing for some secret bit of her soul, and by making him happy, she felt no misgiving whatsoever in taking the coach to spend a week alone away from him.

It probably didn't matter, Trude said, that Murray hadn't arrived at the idea of the Getaway Art Workshop by himself. When she had moved into his place, she had deliberately put in storage all the canvases and other attempts at art she had made over the years. She had put in storage, too, all her books on art, and the notebooks she had kept – either visual diaries or written journals. It was too much, she said, after all those years of living alone, to bring all of herself along when she moved into his house. It was better to keep some of herself separate from him. In fact, that had been the only way she had been able to agree to his suggestion to move in with him. After a few difficult weeks back in her own place, it was either Murray's house or moving back in with our parents, she said, and so it obviously had to be Murray's house. He was a complete stranger to her, no matter what anybody said or surmised about their relationship, but this was all the better for her at the time. It was a clean act of faith, a stepping somewhere else.

As it turned out, of course, it was only with this stranger Murray that she had ever begun to know what love was. In the beginning she hadn't loved him. In fact, she had been repulsed by him and had been suspicious of what people had been saying about him in relation to her. And yet the moment she had decided to side with him on the matter of moving out, she began to realise that he was the one person in the entire world who she could ever be happy with. She hadn't loved him in the beginning and whatever anybody had told me about their relationship, I had to understand that the motivation to avoid our parents had been pivotal in the matter. To have moved back into our parents' house would have been suicide, Trude said, and while the thought of suicide had always been with her – and particularly since the accident – the one of moving back into our parents' house had never been the kind of suicide that she might freely have chosen.

Over the years, she said, she had grown less and less angry with what had happened to her as a child in that house of our parents. Our parents had never intended to hurt or to maim us. They had never actually hurt or maimed us – not our bodies, she said, or at least not to any great extent – but there had been a hurting and a maiming that had taken her years to recover from. After a long time she had become convinced that it had been impossible for our parents to behave in any other way with us than the way they had behaved. They hadn't meant to belittle us or confuse us, she said, or to force us to be covert just to protect the fledgling selves that we couldn't help protecting. Life had been difficult and confusing for our parents in their time and they had been so afraid of this difficulty and confusion that they were always telling us the ways they had found – and ways that they were convinced were effective – of avoiding all the difficulty and confusion that had once befallen them. They were so afraid of the alternative – of this difficulty and confusion – that they never once thought of refraining from telling us what we should do, and instead used all the means available to frighten and coerce us into doing as they said.

For our parents, said Trude, the world was dangerous and devious. At every move, every moment, there was always some evil interest out there to waylay us, to force our heads into the difficulty and confusion they had already experienced themselves. It was so easy to fall foul. We were weak. We were children. Witness, they would say, how as children we believed what our teachers used to tell us, what our friends used to tell us, and what we'd seen on television. We were fools, we were told, because we always believed anything other people said to us. The only ones who could protect us were our parents who loved us. Our parents never meant anything other than an expression of love in what they did to us.

Trude had to believe this was so, but all the same, she said, she could never submit to living with them again. With their love, they would destroy what was left of her. There would be nothing left of her in such an existence, she said, worse than nothing: just a conduit to the difficulties and confusions whose existence, suddenly real, would be all of her self, there being nothing else in the world.

As for Murray, she said, without him – even at the most basic level – she would have died. If he hadn't been there at the accident, she would have died for sure. Without Murray she would have at the very least lapsed quickly into a coma from which she might never have emerged. If Murray hadn't stopped immediately after he'd seen the black four-wheel drive catch the front of her hatchback as it was overtaking, sending her into a spin that finished in the buckled metal barriers along the road, if he hadn't called the police and the ambulance and then reached his hand though the broken glass of her window and begun talking to her just to keep her conscious until the ambulance arrived – Trude had had the story told to her many times, and told the same story to others.

She told the story just to explain the way the nurses kept asking after him when other people were there, as when a colleague from her section at work had come into the hospital with flowers. It was a beautiful story, the colleague had told her. It was romantic. The colleague had especially liked the bit where Murray had insisted that he come into the hospital with Trude because he said that he knew her. That took some cheek, the colleague had said and here she laughed in a way that made Trude feel uncomfortable, because of course Murray had known her a little, at least by sight as far as she had heard (although she hadn't remembered him). He said that they used to go to the same café in Erskineville in the mornings before work (that is, when he used to work at Royal Prince Alfred), and he'd recognised the car because he used to watch her drive off in it whenever he sat at the outside tables, not particularly watching her but noticing who she was all the same. He'd even been thinking about her that morning on the M4 motorway to Penrith, because he had already changed jobs and had begun to miss the days when he only had to drive into the city rather than out west.

All this Trude hadn't told her colleague, partly because she didn't know how she felt about the idea of someone watching her for so many months without her noticing, and partly because she only felt like revealing as much as any of the nurses might have told her colleague otherwise. It was common knowledge that he had waited in the corridor until the first of our family had arrived, and then had stayed with them for the next few hours because, having seen the accident actually happen, he was as good as a television reporter on what had happened and when. And then, as she'd struggled through the confusion of the anaesthetic after one operation and then the other, she was aware, because she'd heard one of our sisters mentioning it, that he had sent her flowers and a funny card with a person completely swathed in bandages on the front of it. He visited her a couple of times, bringing her magazines from the newsagent downstairs in the hospital and once, early on, he had loaded some of his favourite songs onto her iPod.

Our sisters had teased her about him but then they had also been the first to insist, when she had been disturbed by his attentions and didn't want to see him, that she should at least try to listen to what he had to say – that he was a nice man and was obviously infatuated with her.

When Trude came to after the first operation, she heard someone crying very close by. How distressed that person is, she remembered thinking, someone must have died or nearly died. The crying was so close to her, she could hear the tremor of the person's chest as they sucked in the air for the sobs, the congestion of the sinuses, the gumming of fluids. And then she realised that the person crying through the gumming of fluids and swollen sinuses was nobody but herself.

He spoke to her before she'd opened her eyes. She knew he wasn't a stranger, even though she didn't know who he was. She thought that she had dreamed about this person, about this voice, and yet her waking out of the anaesthetic hadn't been out of any dream. There had been some confusion and she remembered there had been a lot of voices, including this voice. She felt anxious, mainly because she couldn't understand what was going on and why nobody wanted to explain anything to her and why there was an immense solidity of pain pushing down on her where she was lying (when it must have been obvious to anybody watching that she would only get crushed as a result of the continuous weight of this pain). She also had a distinct feeling that she had somehow bungled an appointment with some-body by forgetting all the important details she had been entrusted with and that, if only the crushing of her was stopped, she might have a chance to begin thinking about what the important details could have been. She wanted to ask somebody about it, but had no idea how she could even begin to ask any questions. She waited for the crushing to stop and a ground of clarity to take over – for the moment when you realise what it is that you have forgotten and can at least begin to assess what the first thing to do about it might be – and it seemed that at any moment the crushing would stop and this ground of clarity would be about to come.

But then she woke to hear herself sobbing and then his voice. It wasn't out of a dream, but more as if she had just come upon herself by chance, having accidentally wandered away from her body while it had lain confused somewhere else. This effect, she learned later, was only a symptom of the amnesiac component in the anaesthetic, and yet at the time the waking out of not being there had seemed to embody the answer to a mystery that she still couldn't name. The voice she did not recognise was talking to her: You're OK. Don't worry. You're OK. It's all OK.

Morphine was self-administered in the hospital. She liked this, she told me. It gave her some measure of control over her experience of being crushed despite the vomiting of green, yellow and black bile that would inevitably follow. Our sisters came to visit her. Our mother was there nearly every day, bringing newspaper clippings that she raised every now and then from the bedside table, to remind her that they were there (our mother had discovered a few articles on accidents, recovery and the danger of listening to the wrong advice which she thought Trude should read). The flowers in her room stank. One of our sisters, Trude suspected, had given her daisies.

One morning our mother brought up the topic of the man called Murray who, she said, had come in with Trude in the ambulance and had hung around the hospital until after the first operation. Was he somebody she knew well, our mother wanted to find out. Did she know him from work? Trude had shaken her head to indicate she didn't, although she wanted to tread carefully as there continued to be so much that wasn't clear.

She still woke at night into a confusion similar to the one she woke into straight after the operation. In this state, she said, her thoughts were obscure. Even worse: they were not there. It was difficult to describe this, Trude told me, but every time she experienced this confusion it had been the same. She was both thinking and not thinking. It was an absence of thinking. She was frightened by these experiences of thinking and not thinking because she thought that perhaps something had happened to her brain since the accident. In fact afterwards, she told me, she remembered that she had had those same confusions or non-dreams even before the accident. She was pretty sure they weren't dreams – that she was very probably awake for them – but she was so separate from her self at such times that she knew she could neither have been awake nor asleep. It was as if she had died, she thought, or already had gone mad. It was frightening, she told me, but in the end not particularly due to the accident. Since the accident, these experiences had been more pronounced, she said, or perhaps not so much pronounced as more frequent. She had already begun to fear that perhaps her experience was going to be taken over by these confusions – that all she would experience would be these confusions.

When our mother brought up the topic of the man Murray, Trude said, it was terrible to hear that there had been someone else with her just after the accident, and yet reassuring in a way, because some of her confusing experiences had been somehow intertwined with a male voice who had only to be Murray (unless it had been a doctor or a nurse). This man of the voice, who had to have been Murray, hadn't returned since that first day, although fairly soon afterwards our mother told her that he was probably the one who had sent the bunch of blue and yellow flowers and a card, and while Trude didn't know who he was, she no longer trusted herself to know whether she knew him or not.

He came to visit her on the following weekend. One of our sisters was there at the time. You would have to be Murray, this sister had said when he came in and she had stood up in a way that made it clear he might have the chair beside Trude's bed if he wanted it. Trude noticed that he didn't smile. She wondered whether that was because he was by nature a shy or serious person, or that something very wrong had happened – something to do with her – and he had come to clear it up before it went any further. As she still couldn't talk well enough to be understood (there had also, she reminded me, been that trouble with her jaw), she held out her hand to indicate that he might take the chair. Murray, misinterpreting it seemed, took her hand in his. He then gave her hand a slight press and released it. She noticed he had soft, unusually small hands, which were also unexpectedly padded – very unlike the dry, bony hand of our mother. Although Trude hadn't liked having her hand held by our mother, this stranger's hand, she thought, was much more repellent. It had the soft weight of the hand that falls across your chest during the night – a weight that is warm and inert, and which takes you some time to realise is your own.

The sister who was with her had made conversation with Murray. It had been appalling having to listen to it. Several times during the conversation she would have liked to say something, only to steer the conversation away from herself, so they might not continue to talk about her from some innocent belief that people who cannot speak might prefer that people talk about them and their progress very earnestly in their hearing.

Murray had turned a little so that some of the light that was falling through the venetians lit the side of his face. She could see he was a little older than she was. His face was small and he had glassy, pale eyes: somewhat protuberant pale eyes. His brown hair was thinning on the top and he had carefully styled sideburns that had been shaved into a line. He was almost attractive, she'd thought, but at the same time he wasn't at all. He looked gentle and clean, Trude told me, but there was also something repugnant about him – something soft, too quiet, too easily split down the middle. She could see him as an old man, she said. He wasn't old, but she could see him and imagine him as old. Some time later she began to imagine him in a brown checked flannelette dressing gown, bending down to pick up something off the street: a half-smoked cigarette, a flattened beer top that might have looked like a one-dollar coin from a distance. She felt sorry for this old man, this old man who bent over and picked up something from the street, and although she knew that this was no basis for a relationship, she felt sorry for this image of the old man in the street, this old man in a flannelette dressing gown who picked up something from the street, and from then on she couldn't help but be revolted by him, and yet at the same time curious and even mildly attracted.

The first time Trude allowed herself to be taken out by Murray, she made sure it was a film that she wanted to see anyway. He'd suggested the Dendy at Newtown because it was both close and accessible by wheelchair, and rather than trying to work out the mechanics of folding the wheelchair so that he might drive her around to the back of the cinema, it was his idea to push her all the way up the hill himself.

He had come over a couple of times since she'd moved back into her little house in Camperdown. Each time, one of our sisters had been there, or else our mother. Our mother had particularly liked him. He was a nice man, she had said. Why don't you suggest he stay for dinner one evening? Your insurance could pay for some takeaway, surely – this 'surely' being always one of our mother's favourite words when she was attempting to convince us of something that otherwise we might have thought for ourselves.

Of course, the moment our mother expressed this liking for Murray, Trude couldn't see Murray as anything other than a stupid fool that she must have gone out of her way to find for her daughter. All through her life, Trude said, it was only the stupid fools who ever seemed to interest our mother on her behalf. When she was a child in primary school, the son of one of our mother's friends would be the only boy in the class our mother would ask after. How is Paul? she would ask. Is he sitting near you? And when Trude had a birthday party, it was only Paul who had to be invited. Any of the other children in her class could have been exchanged for any other, but Paul was not negotiable. He had to come, Trude said: this Paul whose head was the shape of a television and whose bleating way of speaking, his servile way of continually putting up his hand to answer the most uninteresting of questions in the classroom, annoyed her to the point of screaming. This Paul who became – partly through our mother's constant inquiries as to how he was – the very embodiment of the most stupid fool that it was possible to have in a class and certainly the very last child she might have thought of inviting to her parties. Afterwards, much afterwards, Trude realised that the only reason her mother would have asked after this boy Paul was precisely because of the way that his head was the size of a television and how he was unable to talk without bleating. What was more natural than to be sorry for this boy who had obviously been short-changed in the world and who was very likely the continual concern of his mother (and his mother's friends)?

One day recently, Trude said, she tried to talk about Paul to our mother. She had asked whether there had been something wrong with him and whether this had been the only reason why Trude had been asked to invite him to her parties. And our mother had confessed that it was so and that it had been a terrible worry for her friend, this youngest son. And yet, our mother brightened, this youngest son had actually turned out far better than the two older sons. The eldest son, after coming dux of his primary school and winning the international debating championship in 1987 had become little better than a sponging no-hoper in recent years. This eldest son now always had one scheme after another – he was always only interested in making money – and yet he never stuck to one job or business, let alone one profession, long enough to do anything with it. All of a sudden he would set up a business and then not much later the business would be in receivership and he would be onto something else, but not without a steady injection of funds from his parents. Without his parents, said our mother, the eldest son would have been in prison, or worse: he'd be out on the streets (this son who could argue himself anywhere other than into a good, steady job). The second son was a musician, just a guitarist as our mother would say, and this was quite as bad as the no-hoper.

The youngest son who'd had difficulties as a child was the only one of the three sons who had ever made any good. He worked for the bank, our mother said, and had been so reliable and diligent that several years ago he had become a branch manager in Auburn. The very son who'd had the least opportunities was the one who had turned out the best. Looking on at him when he was a child you might have said there was something wrong with him, said our mother. And it was true. He'd had difficulty learning to talk and even when he could talk he hadn't been comprehensible. Her friend hadn't actually said that there was anything wrong with him, although everybody, said our mother, could see that there was. He was a great worry to his mother when he was young and yet in the end he was the only one who turned out to be anything at all.

All this, said Trude, just confirmed her in the opinion that our mother was not to be trusted. Our mother always had an eye out for such men – such worthy bank manager style men – as if the men who were the least attractive to Trude were the very ones our mother considered to be the most suitable. She imagined our mother taking a train into the city and then a bus out to a slightly classier suburb than the one Trude used to live in – Annandale, or one of the nicer streets in Glebe – our mother walking the lengths of the jacaranda streets as she looked for a well-kept semi-detached terrace with a lonely man inside it. Perhaps he was the hopeless son of one of her many friends. He'd have to be moneyed, steady, but just too diffident to have ever had a relationship with a woman. Don't worry, Trude imagined our mother telling her friend, he just needed a little encouragement. She herself would introduce him to her daughter. Her daughter was free at the moment. That's how it would have been. She would have said she had a daughter who was in hospital. Wouldn't he like to meet her? She had a good little idea: he could pretend that he had come across her wrecked car on the motorway. He could pretend he'd called the ambulance and then waited, talking to her and holding her hand until they came. He could tell her daughter later that he'd come in with her in the ambulance and stayed at the hospital until her first operation was over, just to see that she was all right. Then he could spread this as a rumour. Her daughter wouldn't remember much anyway and what she did remember, he could embroider and contradict. The nursing staff were always ripe for a little gossip. Just tell one of the slightly older nurses, one of the more helpful ones, our mother might have said, and she'd tell everybody else. The hospital was too big and the organisation too chaotic for the story ever to be disproved. She would tell her other daughters the story and as soon as the injured daughter was fully conscious, she, the mother, would then make little suggestions, just enough to get it all going. Some things in this world, she probably concluded to her friend, would never come to fruition if there weren't other people around with the good of everybody at heart. All that was needed was a little help and encouragement. She then might have talked about the family home in Pymble, and the big Christmases with all the other daughters and their families. If he or his mother was still unmoved, she then might have appealed to his sense of adventure or, cunningly, his liking for good ordinary things, like his neat house in Annandale and his four-door Holden Barina hatchback with its box of white tissues on the back seat. She could then have offered a little money: not so much a bribe as a contribution to what she might then have called his 'expenses'.

Whatever means she used, our mother would have been effective, said Trude, and since he had obviously given in – whether after telling himself a few truths or self-justifications, or simply because he was weak, it hardly mattered – Trude could have no respect for the man. Just the sight of him would make her think of inert matter at the bottom of a saucepan: custard, porridge, overcooked pasta, and all of it gone cold and therefore uneaten.

This was the image of the foundling boyfriend that had somehow laid itself over Murray even though he didn't come from Annandale nor drive a small car. It was his eyes particularly that did this for her: their protuberance and their colour. The irises were very pale. Murray had done more looking at her in the hospital than anything else, said Trude, and so she found herself, as soon as she was able to talk again, pushing herself to say things, anything. She'd talked quickly and in short bursts, which was tiring and hurt her jaw. Any time it hurt her to talk in his presence she just allowed herself to close her eyes, deliberately drawing her eyebrows close to the bridge of her nose so that it might be clear that she was in pain. When she felt up to it, she would talk very quickly again. For no reason she would talk about things which, she imagined, might have upset him or at least turned him off her. She talked quickly so she might seem to be somebody who already, without him, had an interesting life. She talked about people who, apart from her sisters, he would never have met. She enjoyed mentioning these other people's names and elaborating on their lives and decisions and, after talking about somebody else for a while, mentioning the first of them again so that he might know how firmly these other people had become wedged into her existence.

As she talked in this way, sometimes with her head turned so that she could look past him, through the venetian blinds and over the disinterested rooftops of other wings in the hospital, sometimes with her eyes directed up towards the cooling white of the ceiling, she would be pursued, in her hurry to explain, by an overwhelming sense of shame. This shame was not so much linked to her awareness of what she was doing by using talk to keep Murray both at a distance and close (almost pressed up against her), but to the memory, nearly twenty years beforehand, of talking quickly to a young man while she was being driven to the Opera House. It was nearly twenty years beforehand, and so she could no longer remember what the young man was like, except for the fact that he had been a few years older than her and she had still not made up her mind whether to like or dislike him. She remembered this other man's bewilderment as he'd stopped the van he was driving before attempting a reverse park in a particularly handy spot in Macquarie Street. He had waited there with the indicator on, as if he wasn't even able to continue parking the van until he could work out why she was talking so much. She was very young then and she knew almost nothing about how any of her thoughts made connections with any other of her thoughts.

She had still, at that time, expected to become an artist, even though she had already allowed herself to enrol in a degree that would soon be exchanged for social work at Sydney University. Many had been the party where she had described to one person after another the story of how her mother had insisted she put arts/law down at university even though she had wanted to go to art school. This, she remembered, had been one of the stories she had told the van driver and, if nothing else, he seemed to believe her (she had become so accomplished at telling the story that she could tell whether people were moved or not).

And yet in the years that followed she had continued with her university studies and, after a shambles of a group art show contribution just after she graduated, she never got round to putting oil paint to canvas again. Her talking, she would come to understand, was her way of giving herself a fiction: and not even so much a fiction of what she might have wanted to believe in but the fiction that came most readily to hand, that hadn't even passed through the filter of her own critical mind. She was like a girl who, when her father wanted to get married again, came across the story of Cinderella and then thought she'd better get down on her knees and scrub the porch.

And so as she talked to the ceiling in the hospital while Murray sat patiently by the bed, the image of the van driver would come to her and, since she had long forgotten what he looked like, she unconsciously found that she was using Murray's features to animate her memory. She saw this Murray–van driver looking at her, his pale, slightly protuberant eyes absorbing the reflections of light from the metal surfaces all around them, his bewilderment now transformed into hurt. She saw him looking out from the Opera House forecourt, the wind raking the green-black water behind him. It was already night and she was no longer there with him. He was alone. Perhaps also, knowing that Murray had supposedly noticed her when she used to drink her coffee by the window in an Erskineville café – watching either from a table further back in the room or even from the café a few shops along the road – knowing that he'd been watching her had simultaneously made her feel a little fearful and guilty and augmented the image of the van driver-come-Murray jilted at the Opera House – the view of the raked waters of the harbour expanding to include the boats sliding slowly towards the shadow under the bridge.

And so, with all this in mind, Trude told me, I should well be able to understand why it was that when Murray arrived at her place some weeks afterwards to take her to the cinema she had mixed feelings. Layers and layers of other people had to be removed before she could get to see this Murray for himself and as he was.

Our sisters had helped her arrange things so that she was able, against the advice of our mother, to stay living for a few weeks in the tiny two-storey terrace she had been renting since the early 'nineties. One sister offered her own sofa bed in place of the old lounge she'd once found on the corner of Mallet Street. Her clothes she hung over the back of her dining chairs or else folded into plastic storage crates and pushed under the table. It always took such a long time to do the most basic of activities. She caught herself thinking of how much Murray would be disappointed in her if he knew how little she was pushing herself, the Murray of this thought having merged now with some ideal sort of Murray, or a Murray who was more like a very ordinary part of herself.

One night with dinner she put on the radio and, just as she sat herself down to eat the omelette she had made, a song came on that she associated with the hospital. It was not a song, though, that she could actually remember hearing there. She hadn't wanted the radio on in the hospital, only the silent show of the television or the occasional lived drama of a movie, and yet she associated that song with the long afternoons of waiting for visitors, as well as the large dark screen of the window at night. She remembered, though, that Murray had wanted to load some songs for her onto her iPod, and she also remembered that he had got her to listen to one or two of them and she had obediently listened to these songs that meant nothing at all to her and were even repellent (all the more so since the listening itself had been an imposition).

It was possible that the song she was hearing in the kitchen was one of those songs, she'd thought. The vocal line was whining and slow in the way she remembered thinking it had been, and the guitar sound was like so many other bands she had heard before and could not name because they had never made any impression on her. It was a west coast band that he liked – the west coast of the United States, that is, not Australia – and yet the very fact that he liked them had made the music sound amateurish and eager, too eager. It was difficult, though, she said, to say that she didn't want him to load the songs, so she had agreed to it, but every time he offered to bring her the iPod she had said she felt too tired and half of her head ached, and when he had gone, she had left it alone. It was the last thing she felt like, listening to music. Even music that she had always liked. Each old song had bound itself to a part of her that she knew had ceased to be since the accident, and even if it was possible still to reinhabit those states, it had felt to her as ridiculous as the idea of wanting to be a child again.

And yet either she had somehow got to hear one of those songs again and become aware that it was a song that Murray had wanted her to listen to, or she had simply remembered it from that first listening and unbeknownst to her, and completely contrary to how she had felt about it, the song had crept into her body in the silent way that fluids are fed through cannulas in a hospital whether you are asleep or awake, because now she experienced the song in an entirely different way to how she had experienced it in the hospital. Although the whine of the vocal line and the insipidity of the guitar seemed as uninteresting, she thought then, as she had experienced them at the hospital, this song, which she now had to associate with Murray, had become transformed into a song whose chords vibrated for long after the song had actually finished. She could not ignore this sure change in her perception of the song. It was good, she now told me, that she did not at all change her original perception of it (its limitations and banality) but found instead that these original perceptions were overlaid by a larger appreciation.

So it was then, she said, that she became sure that this was the same as her ambivalence about Murray: this man who had both repelled her and made her curious and then, as the song still fed through her with the omelette (even after it had stopped playing on the radio), made his own gestures in the voice of the song in her mind (as if Murray had been singing it). This was how, she said, she developed a larger appreciation of Murray, and it was only then that she could see for herself what a miracle it was that they had been brought together after the accident at all. There had never been a moment in her life when she had thought that she would have willingly renounced her independence for anybody else, and much less someone as unappealing as he had first seemed to be.

I should know, she reminded me, what she had been like with her first boyfriends. The moment they became anxious about her – the moment they had suggested that they see her every day – she had been unable to control an overwhelming antipathy. Until the moment of their statement of emotional dependence, she would be infatuated with them (or if not infatuated, at least very willing to see them), and yet after this point (this break) she would be unable to think of them in any other way than with antipathy and dread.

She had grown used to this reaction in herself over the years, and so had come to accept that she had not been made to live with anybody else, unless it was someone who didn't care whether they saw her or not. She had never found this perfect kind of person, who was both attractive enough to want to be with and uncaring enough not to mind whether they saw each other every day. There should have been plenty of people in the world like that, she used to think, but she had never met any of them. Television and films seemed to proliferate with people of this sort, and yet she had never found anyone in the real world who measured up to this ideal.

Sometimes, she said, she would meet someone who seemed to be sufficiently self-obsessed to measure up to this standard, but invariably, these same people would drive her mad with all their little games, their attempts to fish for responses from her all the time. It was bizarre, she said, that Murray had eventually got past all those barriers in her, all those barriers she had erected through her years of experience. He might have reminded her of the most pathetic of her times with men as a young woman, but this in itself should not have been enough to get past the barriers around her heart. In the end it was just something unconscious, she said, and hence in its way nothing short of a miracle. Plenty of people had bandied about the term 'miracle' but only with Murray and the art workshop did it make any sense.

It would have been good to ring Murray that night in the pub up the coast, and it wasn't that she forgot, at least not completely. All the time at the Getaway Art Workshop he had been far enough away and yet as connected to her as if he was holding the end of a long piece of string that she had loosened to its farthest extent. At the Getaway Art Workshop she was as far away from him as it was possible to get without breaking the string entirely. Although she hadn't quite forgiven him for going behind her back and colluding with our mother, neither was she still angry with him any more.

Trude suspected that when Murray had talked to our mother behind her back, he'd probably only had a very innocent reason to ring her. Murray, she said, wasn't a particularly sneaky or malicious person. She couldn't imagine him ringing our mother just to talk about her – she didn't believe that. And yet he was hopeless, she said. He had no idea about our mother. For someone who had to deal with the most gruesome realities – namely the long-term effects of injuries and trauma as part of his work as a physiotherapist every day – who had to talk through recovery plans with people who had seen the whole side of their leg sliced away in an industrial accident – he was particularly naïve when it came to our mother. When our mother, for example, asked after something in her bright little voice, Murray would never have suspected any ulterior motive for that bright little voice and would very likely have given in the simplest and most candid way possible any details that had been requested.

Our mother, she thought, must have asked whether she was drawing. Perhaps Murray had only rung our mother to ask after some details about a family get-together. Perhaps she had rung him. Whatever had been the impetus for the phone call, our mother would have made sure that any questions she wanted to ask him were ready by the phone. It would have been handy for our mother that it was only Murray on the phone because then, Trude suspected, she needn't have had to be as careful in how she asked these questions. There might have been a question about children – although, since the accident, it was likely that our mother would have given up on Trude having children – but the question of art would, of course, have been raised. Trude had a man, our mother might have thought, and so now she had every opportunity to be able to pursue her art.

Although our mother had tried to bring up the efficacy of art as an aid to recovery, all the time Trude could tell that the most important thing in the scheme of things was that there was a man who seemed to be interested in her daughter (which in reality meant at last Trude was interested in a man and settling down). Didn't you know she was good at art? our mother would have asked, the intonation rising very high at the end of the question, as if she had been genuinely surprised that he didn't know (which would have been true) and as if this response had been artless and spontaneous (which could never have been the case).

Murray would have received the information about Trude's art with genuine surprise. He was quite behind our mother, he later told Trude, in trying to encourage her to get back into her art. He could see that it hadn't really been possible before the accident. Trude's job had taken over her, as jobs take over everyone. He said he owed it to Trude and to our mother to make sure that her art didn't languish, as everything else in her life, of necessity, had had to languish. Since the accident, he said, she could go either one way or the other. In his work he saw how people coped with pain and disability and either this catalysed a new energy in a person – an unusual energy and optimism – or else everything fell apart, first one thing and then another. If there was one thing he could offer, he said, it would be to do what he could for her emotional life. He didn't want to step on the toes of the professionals she already had to deal with, but as a partner and friend he could support and encourage her.

Murray could be pompous, Trude remembered, whenever he talked about himself as a partner and friend. He had a way, too, of blinking when he said it, as well as a certain irritation, as if he could already tell that she didn't like to hear him talking about himself in this way, but continued to do so because he thought it was important.

She had not forgotten about Murray at the little pub in town, but Dave had distracted her and then there hadn't been much time to do anything about ringing him. Once or twice early on, she had thought of asking about whether there was a pay phone in the hotel or up the street. When they had all walked through the bar behind William on their way to the corridor, she should have looked out for one of those small orange or blue pay phones but she hadn't remembered just then. Quite apart from Dave, it was also very likely the effect of the bottle shop door sliding shut that had made her thoughts turn inwards rather than outwards onto what she should have been doing next. Without the effect of that door, she might have followed through on ringing Murray.

When the travellers from the workshop had been allocated their rooms upstairs by William, there had been a lot to do to prepare the beds because all the mattresses were bare and some of the rooms were still covered with drop sheets and newspaper. Trude managed to avoid the work that the others had to do, but it was not possible to avoid going upstairs along with them. It was very dusty upstairs and some of the rooms smelt too strongly of paint to use but as Monique had said, it was fantastic being able to stay in such a place, such an authentic old pub, and wasn't it a bargain et cetera. But all the time, Trude said, while the others were making the beds and talking, she found herself still thinking about the sliding door and what it had to mean. She felt herself to be filling up with thoughts of the impending disaster or urgent and life-changing choice that had already been decided for her by the simple collusion of her body and the door.

After the bustle of getting the rooms ready was over, she lay on her bed and waited until it was time to go down to dinner. On the other side of the wall she could hear the shuffling feet of Sidney, the fat man, and the occasional thud or sliding, dull rattling sounds of what must have been the twin to the set of drawers with broken pendulous handles that had been pushed up against the wardrobe in the room that Trude had been given. It was a small room with a high window of smeared grey glass. Since it was right next door to the men's bathroom, Trude wondered whether, in an earlier time, the room might have been intended as a linen closet or a storeroom for brooms and other cleaning equipment. Neither Dave nor his brother had evidently been up this end of the corridor with their tins of paint. The walls were a yellowish cream and in places had the texture of grapefruit skin. In the corner, to one side of the window, the paint was peeling off in dramatic furls, revealing plaster that buckled and cracked. All in all, however, she liked the room. It reminded her of the old house that our grandmother had lived in until the time of her stroke and hospitalisation: a house which, despite the basic refurbishment that our mother had given it after our grandmother's death (a coating of paint, wall-to-wall carpet, and tiling in the bathroom), continued to exist, for Trude, in its earlier form.

When Trude was shown the room by Grace after the bed had been made, her first thought had been to lie down and try to get some rest before the dinner was served. This she did, without even taking off her shoes. The bed was high and swung creakily to one side as she climbed onto it, but elevated in this way and with the taut chenille bedspread barely dented by her presence on it, she felt momentarily not so much stable as weightless and reduced: shrunken somehow to the body of a child.

Although she was able to lie very still, the weightlessness of her body made it impossible to doze. Her thoughts, with her body, held themselves out from her, and worse, they constantly moved and tangled with each other.

The feeling of inexplicable dire or urgent consequences that she had felt in relation to the sliding to of the bottle shop doors was still there while she was resting. It was an irrational mood that had come over her. She began to wonder whether it was not so much the superstition of the door sliding closed but the whole context of the afternoon and the pub they had found themselves in that had made it so easy to succumb to this mood. With this mood, she said, the seemingly infinite optimism that the others had come away with from the workshop (and which had affected her just a little, at least for a while), this optimism had been stifled. Or if not stifled – because of the additional sense that it was only she that might be expected to make a life-changing choice, and that this choice might be the best choice she had ever had to make in her life – if not stifled, then contained very securely.

Even the fact that she had started drawing again at that Getaway Art Workshop meant nothing for the moment other than the realisation that she would have to get off the bed and look once more at the pictures she had brought away with her before she could decide whether the sketches were anything other than an embarrassingly overworked connection of lines.

She also thought, at a small distance from these other thoughts, about how hard her mother had been working to get her to start drawing again, or more specifically, to take up again what she'd liked to term 'portraiture'. Trude had once been so good at it, and it was a terrible shame not to take the opportunity, now she was settled, to put the word about.

Despite these discouragements, though, there was something about the image of the door, something she knew she could trust. She knew I would be cynical – I was the cynical one, she thought; she had always noticed this about me – but the fact was that she had been overtaken by this image and she knew in the guts of her that she wasn't being misled.

It was then, while she was lying there thinking of her mother, that she had the most determined thought that she should ring Murray to tell him not to drive out to the coach terminus to meet her that night. It was a good time to ring Murray, she knew, so long as she could find a phone to ring him from. She stretched her hands out along the chenille coverlet. For a moment, she had a very strong sense that Murray might have been thinking about her. She saw his head slightly tilted, looking down at her (which was surprising, since he was barely a centimetre taller than she was), a look of concern on his face – or at least his eyes were luminous and he wasn't speaking. Murray had the kind of eyes which seemed to be able to suggest, at the same time, both her own thoughts as well as those she interpreted to be his. Part of this effect probably came from the way that his eyeballs, by protruding a little above the lower lid, took in reflections from more than a hundred and eighty degrees. It was always as if he was able to see, simultaneously, everything that lay on either side of him, that was coming up from beneath him, and even, or so it seemed to Trude, that was only beginning to take form in his new partner's mind. It was this suggestion that he knew what she was thinking that made Trude unwilling to look back into his eyes whenever he was looking at her. At such times, Trude knew, she must look like someone who is evasive because she has something to hide and so, even as she had to look away from him (over the dinner table, for example, and in bed) she would, without fail, find herself casting around in her mind for something to talk about, and if she couldn't think of anything to talk about, beginning, just a little, to panic.

She thought of what she would say to him now, the very words delivered fast, so she wouldn't hear the questioning silence he often sent back at her over the phone: Hi, Murray, I'm ringing from this old hotel. Listen, there was a storm up this way and we were delayed getting out to the town where the coach leaves from, so we're all having to stay the night so that we can be on the next one. The words, her words, would of course get him walking around the room. She would imagine him on the other end walking around the kitchen with the phone held to his ear (the fingers of one hand splayed evenly across the plastic) and the other hand tugging here at a towel on the oven rail, there at a bill from under a pile of papers (little jobs that he might have done at any other time but that he particularly seemed to reserve for telephone conversations).

The image of his face, though, unclear as it was except for the three dimensions of his eyes, was so strong that she felt a strong, sure pulling on the bony part of her chest, and rather than thinking of him walking back and forth on the small wooden floor of the kitchen, she saw him opening the back door to go and sit in the garden. This image of him outside in his garden, with the interior lights from the windows illuminating the pathos of the sparse hair on his scalp, gave Trude such a sudden spasm in the muscles around her heart that she was convinced that there was something specific that she had promised to do in relation to him, something essential and more important than just telephoning him with her whereabouts.

She became rigid on the chenille bed covering, and she knew that if she turned over onto it so that her face pressed into it, the oily, faintly cigarette-scented bobbles in the ridging would make her believe that she had begun an entirely strange life somewhere else, far from everyone that she knew, and on her own. It was perhaps this feeling that had come upon her in the room while she waited for the time that they had all agreed to have dinner downstairs with William – this feeling that she had become a stranger – which first clarified the confusion of thoughts that had come to her after she had failed to get through the bottle shop door before it shut and made it possible for her to begin to believe that she had actually passed through rather than been stopped by a barrier; that she had misread the sign of the door.

Trude tapped on the plastic table to get my attention. The roofs were still bright across the road but the sky had been leached to the colour of glass. I had been staring at this scene as she was talking to me – staring but taking nothing of it in, or so I thought – but now I realised that all the time she had been talking, I had been noticing the way the light was defining the meticulous corrugations in the roofs on the shops opposite, all the rusted parts of the capping and the irregularities in the flashing around a chimney whose render was in disrepair (my fascination with the revelations of the roofs and the chimneys becoming intertwined with the circuitous nature of what Trude had been telling me).

This had always happened to me, I realised. Whenever Trude tried to tell me something – even when I was much younger and wasn't yet aware of the ambiguities in my attitude to both her and what she was trying to tell me – I never looked at her as she was talking to me but instead became transfixed by the details of wherever I was. My mind would follow what she said, one word after another, but my eyes would have been following the patterns of something else. While she was telling me about one of her friends, and this friend's opinions, for example, I would be following the patterned disorder of the bookcase in my room. This was not to say that I ever found boring what Trude had to tell me. Far from it. And yet it would be impossible for me to watch her as she spoke; to watch her as she spoke would have been to divert her (I seemed to realise) so that her train of thought might have turned and been aimed in my direction. Much as I had always longed for her trains of thought to be aimed in my direction, I also realised that I wouldn't have been able to withstand the result; that the very (unconscious) thought of her aiming a train of thought in my direction was already to experience a painful interrogation. I could only withstand her trains of thought, I realised, by allowing them to pass by me as I listened, passing by me, for example, into the uneven vertical layering of books in my bookcase. I looked out as I listened then, my listening becoming the looking (the looking as an attempt to withstand being a listener, by remaining only a listener).

And yet Trude seemed to guess what I was doing. She had called me a cynic; if only that were true. I was not so much a cynic as a coward, I realised. If I hated her as much as I was only beginning to realise, I might have made a stand, as she herself might have described it. I might indeed have tried to turn the conversation around. I had been away from Australia for years – long years during which she had never once enquired about how I was or what I was doing, or so I had heard from our mother. I had heard, too, that she had been jealous of the fact that I had been living in France and was able to speak French. She could speak French, she would say, quite as well as I had ever done when I was still in Australia. In fact, she had been a better speaker of French at high school (or so I heard from our mother), and all that without the advantage of being surrounded by the language. Had she brought up the question of her proficiency in French, I could have said that there had been nothing to prevent her from travelling to France as I had done and becoming better at French than I ever could be. There had been no reason for her not to travel to France – no relationship, no job, no commitment that might have prevented her.

All this I could have told her. It was ready inside me. My head was ringing with the words and the arguments that I was going to use with her. But when Trude tapped on the plastic table, I had looked at her briefly (my response had been automatic). I didn't try to turn the conversation around but instead allowed my gaze to wander over her shoulder to a single line of crumbling in the mortar behind her. It was at this moment that I wondered at what a coward I was. I might have smiled as I realised this, because she responded as if I had encouraged her. She shifted forwards in her chair across the plastic table between us. Her eyes were avoiding mine, I was sure, as much as mine were also avoiding hers.

Whatever I thought about where she was living and what she was doing (or not doing – she knew what I was thinking), Trude said that I had to understand how important it was for her to have been waylaid at that pub up north, as our mother had put it. It was typical, she told me, that the moment that she found her true calling in life – however close it might have been to an ideal our mother might have already formed for her – that this true calling had become an object to be picked apart and worried over.

Our mother had envisaged that she take up her portraiture again within the comfort of her new home. People could come to her. She could advertise in the local paper and through word of mouth. Even more than her disappointment that Trude had seemed to be abandoning dear Murray had been her utter horror to hear that, within a month or so of returning from up north, Trude had moved out from her new home into a pub where all sorts of people came. No one in their right mind would think of making such a move so soon after an accident, our mother had said, and if she thought she had moved out to further her art, she was simply being fooled by the kinds of ideas those hippies up north were always trying to fool people with. Nothing was further from being conducive to art than moving into such a disgusting place as a local pub where all manner of people hung out at all hours. Nobody would want to come to a pub to get their portrait painted, she had said. Trude was out of her mind to think otherwise.

In the light of such opposition, Trude said I had to believe how important her decision to move had been. There had never been a moment in her life when she had been surer that she had done the right thing by moving out of Murray's and moving in here. The crux of it had come to her at that pub up north. She had begun to draw – to really draw – at that pub that evening. She had begun to draw properly, in the way she had always wanted to draw. She had become immersed in her drawing – thinking of nothing else but her drawing – and yet in the background of this had been a clamour of people talking – even a concatenation of voices – which in normal circumstances had always worked against the possibility of being able to draw well.

All these years, she said, she'd thought it impossible to concentrate on her drawing, let alone dedicate herself to her drawing as she had always wanted to do as a child, because the clamour of worries always made it too difficult to concentrate on her art. All these years she had thought that the barrier to achieving her goals was impassable because it was too high and she was too weak. She would have to stop working for money first, she used to think, because only then could she concentrate on what she wanted to do. She had to stop working for money and yet, somehow – this 'somehow' being unreal to her – still have enough money to be able to live doing her art. Several times this had been within reach (that is, she had been made redundant), but each time she couldn't resist looking for a new job for herself. There had always been this panic, this anxiety, that unless she found a new job, all the best things about her circumstances would begin to fray all around her and she would have to move out of her house and back into our parents' house, which was impossible, she said. Or else she would have to move out to the country, to a house she could afford to live in on the dole – and yet the very thought of moving out to the country had always filled her with dread and made her think of dead grass and rusty car parts and lonely, fly spotted plates under a too hot sun.

All these thoughts up until that evening in the pub up north had been nothing but barriers. There was no way she was ever going to achieve what she wanted in life if she continued to think in this dream-denigrating way. But by thinking of herself as a stranger, she said, her life had become very simple. She was convinced something had already happened to her – all she had to do was be patient and she would know what to do. Murray, she expected, would soon grow used to it. She knew Murray was right for her, and so this couldn't be incompatible with still seeing him now and then. He was an intuitive man and was already beginning to understand why it was she had left him. She could see that our mother had no idea what she was talking about when she raved on and on in her usual way.

So it was, said Trude, that as she got off the bed after her rest and made her way downstairs to the small room behind the bar where dinner was being served, she felt herself to be as insubstantial as a figure on a screen. It was her first taste of freedom, a freedom that was real. She had already described this to Murray and although he had argued with her, even shouted at her near the end, he seemed to know what she was talking about. That was the thing about Murray, he could always understand.

When she entered that little room behind the bar, she had the feeling that she was walking into a scene she had walked into before. Even the way that it was lit – with a series of those old 'sixties lamps on turned wooden stands – gave the impression that she had already counted the lamp bases and assessed the greasiness of the lampshades on another occasion that she could no longer remember. Sausages and salad had been served on plates on a pair of tables pushed together in the centre of the room, and the travellers from the Getaway Art Workshop were sitting on chairs with their backs to the wall.

Trude didn't remember how the meal had started, but she knew she didn't talk for some time. If she had been reticent at the art workshop, it was nothing to this detachment that had come over her that evening at the pub. But while at the art workshop she hadn't bothered noticing anything of the conversations that had gone on around her, she now found herself interested in everything she heard. If I could understand what she meant, she could try describing what was happening to her as being like someone waking up to find herself in the middle of a film. The film had already started and so the set-up was over. She had no idea who she was or who she was meant to be, but everything was significant as it can only be in films.

It was while they were all eating the food that William had brought for them that he commented on the fact that one of them was late. His brother, William said, had reminded him that there had been five travellers, which he might have known for himself but hadn't bothered counting until now. It was less likely that his brother Dave would have got the number wrong (Dave had been a teacher of maths, and so getting a number wrong would have been sublimely embarrassing) than that somebody was intentionally avoiding the meal which he had slaved *tout le soir* to prepare. The sausages had been hand-picked. Even the salad he had raised himself – or at least the rocket, which was already eaten (he was very sorry he had eaten it, but there had only been a few leaves).

William then started to ask about the fat man. It was extraordinary, he said, that of all the people he might have expected to go on an art camp – and one of those art camps, what was more, that were located in less than comfortable settings – that of all people, the fat man struck him as the very person least likely to have put himself to the bother and expense of going. William was curious about people who wanted to go on art camps. Most people were too stuck in their ruts to bother with such a thing, and the older they got, the more likely that they needed a particular kind of lever to prise them from the small place that their arse cheeks were stuck in. He was therefore very surprised that the fat man had achieved this. No one was to laugh. He wasn't trying to be funny. In fact, he would go as far as saying that, although he was surprised that the fat man had had the gumption to get himself off his commodious butt and out into the countryside here for no other reason than to embarrass himself, it was also likely that he was the very one with the most carefully developed talent for it. Wide-eyed inno-cence was probably the only requisite: wide-eyed innocence and blinkers like *les murs*. The rest, he would say, was simply dressing up.

Some people, he knew, spent months if not years of their lives preparing themselves for such an art camp, in the way that four-year-olds putting on tiaras and plastic pearls will believe they are going to be queens one day. Their so-called 'funky haircuts', piercings and layered singlet tops would have come before and not after they had decided to go on an art camp. First of all, he said, they would have had to feel themselves in the part (*comme il faut*), which meant experimenting with their haircuts and clothes.

In this respect at least, the fat man could be excused from any superfi-cial toe-twirling. It was very likely, William thought, that their fat friend would have known from the outset that there was nothing he could do about being the artist he was and so had spent years trying to stifle this fact with his choice style of clothing. In fact he was as likely to have been born an artist in the same way as his body had been built to carry that weight: a veritable Van Gogh with a little more *je ne sais quoi*.

And so it started, said Trude: a discussion about being an artist. William had begun and it rolled forwards from there. It had been all she had been thinking about and trying to understand for herself; the very discussion that she both wanted and dreaded to have happen at the Getaway Art Workshop.

At William's suggestion that the fat man might have been born an artist, a discussion got under way about whether this was possible: not so much about the fat man per se but about whether anybody could be born an artist (or indeed into any particular job or profession at all). It was the issue which was behind everything they had done at the Getaway Art Workshop; everything they had done and everything they had said, but it took somebody like William to speak out with the obvious. A couple of the others then said a few things.

Trude didn't pay much attention to the beginning of the discussion. All she remembered was that the beginning of the discussion had deviated from a discussion about being an artist to the notion of fate and the lines on people's hands. It had deviated very quickly and so she had soon lost concentration. Also, at the beginning of the discussion, she had been too preoccupied with the gristle in the sausages and her attempts to see whether there was any tomato in the salad (she had always been allergic to tomato, I should remember).

Soon she noticed that the conversation had come back to the fat man again. Jay had been saying something about the way she thought her father should have been a piano tuner rather than the accountant that he was, and then she had gone on to defend Sidney the fat man as someone who was at least taking risks and listening to his heart in the way her father had never done. As for artistic potential, she then moved on to say that this idea was more difficult to judge (more difficult, for example, than noticing how much better her father would have been as a piano tuner than an accountant), but as far as she could tell, Grace was the only one she had ever met with artistic potential. It was clear as daylight during the workshop. You just had to see how she composed her pictures. Grace didn't approach her work like anyone she had ever met before. Sure, said Jay, Grace could be easily flustered and would say things at the sharing sessions that even sounded dumb, they were that obvious (and here she purposely avoided looking at her new friend), but it had been refreshing hearing these things said all the same, since no one else was game enough to say them – things like art needing to make a statement or pose a question. Truly obvious things. She had a lot in her, this Grace. She only needed to relax and open up. Coming back to the fat man, Jay then said she didn't want to denigrate Sidney. She had the greatest admiration for this larger than usual man, Sidney. He was obviously way out of his element up here. It couldn't have been easy coming here all by himself. God, she said, they should have seen the way he laboured over a lemon that first day when the rest of them were still out doing the path perspectives. It was awful, this lemon. You'd have thought the lemon had had a skin five centimetres thick, it looked that hard and concrete and dead when he did it, but all the same it was sweet. She thought it was sweet that Sidney had thought of enrolling. Some people like Sidney usually never got the nerve to test out what they could do.

It was at this point, of course, that Sidney entered the room. The timing was embarrassing, but nobody else seemed to realise it. Although he was a fat man, Trude reminded me – in fact an unusually large fat man – the way he moved into the room made you think of something small. Nobody had actually been directly cruel about Sidney, but she knew something would have been noticeable in the ambience of the room. It was impossible for him not to notice that people had been talking about him. He would have been an idiot not to notice this. But as far as she could see, he didn't seem to notice anything. When he opened the door he had turned round so that his rounded back was facing the others. He then seemed to busy himself in the closing of the door. He was busy with the door in the way of someone who sees their whole existence as a series of similar small acts of completion. While this might have been a ploy to hide his embarrassment, it was very difficult to believe this when you watched him at the door handle.

There was something about seeing someone in this position which made it hard to sympathise with them, said Trude. Until the moment he had come into the room, she had felt protective of Sidney. Even Jay had been protective of the fat man, Sidney, in her way. At the art workshop he had always been there doing his lemons and other kinds of fruit, and Trude had found herself becoming amused at his doggedness and seeming imperviousness to criticism (several times it had been suggested, to no avail, that he try working on something different or changing his technique). But seeing him fiddling at the door handle after entering the room – and entering the room in the middle of such a potentially very embarrassing situation – seeing him fiddling in this way had made her begin to wonder about his intelligence and this made it all the easier not to worry about what he was thinking.

She wanted to tell me this now, she said, just so I could understand the context of the evening. It was really a very minor aspect of the evening, but if she didn't tell me about it I might get the wrong idea about the way that this fat man, Sidney, could not help but come across.

After finishing with the door handle, Sidney turned around with a little smile on his face, a smile which only confirmed Trude in her thoughts about the emptiness of his mind. For a few moments he turned to one side and then another as if he didn't know where he needed to stand or where to turn his eyes. Interestingly, it was then, she said, that looking from William to Sidney and Sidney to William that she realised that Sidney was no more a fat man than William was. They were both large men. In fact, William was taller than Sidney and, given this, with his corresponding bulk, was probably even heavier than Sidney might have been. And yet still, as she looked at both of them, she could see that one was the fat man and the other was William.

William had got up out of his chair when Sidney approached the table. He wanted Sidney to help himself and his thick freckled arm had gestured wide towards what was left of the sausages and salad. Everyone was watching the fat man, Trude said. His face was shiny. Thin wisps of dark hair over his ears had flattened into whorls against the damp of his skull. He kept open-ing his mouth, making a little gasp, and then closing it again, as if he was always about to say something but kept changing his mind. Trude thought that he was looking at her, but when she looked back at him she saw that he was not focusing on her but somewhere about a metre back from where she was standing. It was terrible having to watch him like this, this man who had been the topic of a conversation he had missed.

William, who had started it all, had then attempted to save the situation. He told Sidney that they had been talking about art and that he had been fascinated, absolutely fascinated by what he had been hearing. He said that they were wondering whether Sidney had any opinion about who had the greater talent – at least among those present. They weren't to bother about the people who hadn't even thought of coming to stay *chez nous*, as he put it. He suggested that they not bother at all about them.

Sidney the fat man had then sat down in a chair at the table next to Trude. He had that look of someone, she thought, who always assumes that conversations are what other people engage in. He was avoiding responding to William, whether by design or by omission. Either he was a complete idiot, she'd thought then, or an extremely shrewd man. It was hard to tell at this point. He was very well disguised.

When the fat man sat down, he soon began to help himself from the table. He was making little sounds as he moved around the food: the slight movement of a plate on wood, the singing friction of cutlery, even smaller unnameable fabric or body or thought sounds, as of someone settling themselves into a situation.

Perhaps it was these smaller sounds which had got to William, making him determined to press on. He wanted to involve his friend Sidney, he said, in a project to help his brother Dave get off his arse and do something. In fact, all of them could help him, he said, since they were evidently all such creative and interesting types. He said he liked it that they had come here unannounced, disrupting their lives and throwing his brother into a panic. Something had to be done about the situation, and this disruption had been the ideal beginning. He was supposed to be helping with the painting of the hotel, but his *frère* Dave had refused to let him touch it. Dave didn't know what he was missing, as William had quite a touch with colour. He didn't at all take to Dave's idea of sticking with the heritage palette. They were all creative and he wished Dave would think of asking their opinions.

In fact, he would love to see what Dave, his dear brother Davie, would do if they just confronted him and asked him to explain himself and his plans for the hotel. They were artists, he said, and so they could do this. They had to be brave. He would like that: to see how Dave would cope if they talked to him about this room for instance. God knew what he would do, what he would think (this *frère extraordinaire* of his). Dave wouldn't tell him of course. He wouldn't be able to see what was going through Dave's mind. William wouldn't be able to hear what calamities were sending out their gigantic sounds, because it would all be in his brother Dave's head. It all only stayed and was locked, even forgotten, in Dave's head. He knew his brother, William said. He knew how he could close on anything. Even so, there would be perceptible differences in what he did as a result of a little careful prompting. Dave, usually, was entirely predictable. William said he could set Dave down in a room and his little hairy legs would already be moving before they reached the floor. He could wind up Dave and face him in one direction. Dave would move this way and then that way. This way and then that way. But a Dave with something else roaring silently in his head might just not whirr that way entirely in a whirring way. William would love to see that. He thought he could spot it at once. He wanted them all to do this little creative, very daring little thing. He called them his dearest artists. He would be very, very grateful for this, he said.

When William stopped talking, Trude could hear the small sounds Sidney made as he ate. They were not only the usual sounds of mastication and swallowing but, every now and then, small notes that came from his throat, that might have been the sounds of someone clearing their windpipe. It was as if, while he was eating, the fat man was continually testing that his voice wasn't gravelly, that he would be able to start talking the moment that he wanted to talk. There was also a sense, from these noises, that he was simply signalling that he was appreciative of the food and would have liked to say something about it but couldn't yet think of exactly what he wanted to say. As well as making these little noises in his throat, the fat man continually shifted himself on his chair: again, the movements were very small and were expressive of some desire to communicate with the others in the room with him, or perhaps only William.

Trude found that these sounds, as well as the mastication, and the movements which she not so much saw as felt, were impossible to ignore. She thought that the fat man wanted a response to these small initiatives of his, or at least, if he didn't quite directly want them, he would have liked them very much. In fact, she thought, he deserved to have some kind of response, only in the sense that any person who has joined a group of people for a meal (and by their implied invitation), surely deserved as a measure of human respect to be given some response to any attempts they might make at communication.

For this very reason, Trude was so irritated by the seemingly demanding but harmless presence of the fat man that she neither looked at the fat man nor at the others. She looked, instead, at the empty plate in front of her, and to distract herself from the thought of her response being unreasonable and even irrationally unkind, she looked hard and dispassionately at the contours of the plate and for the first time in her life (she had never been into still lives, she now explained to me), she could see how it was that someone might want to capture the pregnant, irrefutable and confident stillness of a plate.

It was into this moment of awkwardness that Monique had spoken. Since William had raised it, she thought they all should look a little closer at what he had been saying. He had kept using the word 'creative' as if they all knew what he meant, but it was obvious that they didn't and neither did he. She herself couldn't stand the way everyone used the words 'creative' and 'creativity' as if they knew what they were talking about.

All it meant, she thought, was an action that was a little different from any other actions: more daring or more to the point – and she thought this was always the intended meaning – just to get the fuck out of someone else's brain for the moment – and do something, anything – because the person who was speaking was always up to their eyebrows in their own much more fucking important worries. That is, creativity just meant do it yourself, like get on the job and make your own decisions for bloody once. That was the definition, at least that was the definition they all had to live with from one day to the next.

And then there was the other definition: the airy-fairy-I'm-important creativity. The might-I-be-one-of-the-elect-and-twirl-on-my-toes creativity. This was the definition that sucked them all in, Monique thought. If it were dangled in front of them, they would step off a precipice for it. Fork out the thousands of dollars so long as it was for creativity and everyone was sweet, most especially the suckers they were.

And so, given this, she then said, she was sure they were all wondering why it was that she had enrolled in the Getaway fucking Art Workshop? Did they think that was the reason? Fuck their arses it wasn't, she said. She wasn't thinking about anything so arse-stupid as creativity when she filled out that form online and typed in her credit card numbers and sent it off on that pale blue site with all those fucking stupid gum leaves whirling like insects in the corners of it.

The way she saw it, there were the gullible and the not so gullible. William was to correct her if she was wrong, but it seemed to her that Dave didn't know much about what was going on around the hotel. Was she right? He just did his stuff. Worked at the renovating, watched over the bar staff. He didn't even look as if he'd been attempting to pull in many clients. He was the kind of person who kept on and on at his renovating precisely so that he could avoid having people in to stay. They all could even be the very first people he'd had to stay in the hotel, renovations or no, and if it hadn't been for William's suggesting it, Dave would never even have thought of offering. It seemed to her that he'd got the money, but not any particular know how. Or she should say he'd just got this dream in the way that all sorts of small kinds of pen-pushers and hack workers – and, yes, 'yes workers' (I'll go on that tedious trip for you, boss; I'll stay back late for you, boss; her ex-husband was one of those) – all these men of limited ideas (and for the most part, she thought, these kinds of workers were men) suddenly took it into their heads that, after all those years of licking boot tops and keeping their ties very straight (*very* straight!), a certain kind of thing existed out there which they could buy (it was usually only something that they could buy, which someone – some mate of theirs – had tried to sell them) and this thing was all of a sudden, and quite entirely, the only embodiment of beauty that they could get their small minds to comprehend. Everything they then said was only in justification for what it was they had decided to call beautiful, or should she say real or even the only thing worth going for, the only way to live.

Her ex, after one of those times he'd called in to see an old university mate in Newcastle, had got this thing about boats. Suddenly all there was in his universe was the world of the land and the world of boats and water. The world of the land was all 'bad', and that included everything on land (the family house, his work, his children, their friends, any films that weren't about water or boats, all books that had nothing to do with either fishing or sailing or marine life). It wasn't that he used the word 'bad' in fact. He was subtler than that. His years of hardly saying anything had caught up with him suddenly in a flood of descriptions of how his work tied him into this lifestyle of crawling along dead roads to see that certain dead marketing ploys got put into action. Everybody, he would say, was tied into this impossible set of relationships which had them all hardly moving or, if moving, only moving in useless, dead parodies of freedom. The sea, he said, was completely filled with life, and was also, as his ex was supposed to know well from certain documentaries, the origin of all life. Everything existed in potential in the ocean and therefore everything of life was in there all the time. In fact, so he said, there was never any one place in the ocean where one thing could exist and, by existing, exclude something else from existing as well. If we could all fly, he'd say, we'd have been happier animals, the air becoming a near replacement for the sea. If we could have flown, there would never have been imposed on us any of these ridiculous strictures, these arbitrary and rigid relationships.

When he talked like this, Monique would try to point out that they didn't have gills and so there was no way that they could survive beyond a single breath in that ocean he loved. Even if he did one of those diving courses and got himself rubber skin and a tin of air, that skin and air would only last until the end of their use-bys. And what's more, she would say, even if he had gills and sprouted flippers, she wondered how he would like it if in the first fifteen seconds of his ocean freedom, the seemingly endless but in fact very contained infinity of this precious bloody ocean of his, some shark nudged up to him with its multiple set of wire-sharp teeth, the teeth hooking in on his newly liberated flesh. Even if it didn't want to eat him then, she would say, those wire-sharp teeth would have hooked him and the blood leaking from his thigh would have brought a roiling mass of predators, the sea churning under him with the feeding on the animal that was himself.

And did any of those listening, Monique wanted to know, understand what the stupid thing was? Did they know what the thing was that defied comprehension about this man? Nothing that she said made him in any way less determined to see the world in the way he was seeing it. Standing back from him – when she was away from him at work or just in another room, it being only five or ten minutes before he would open his mouth to talk to her again – she would still be convinced that the bullshit he was talking about was only that: indescribable, laughable bullshit. So fucking stupid did it seem that she only had to mention one thing or question one small detail and everything, the whole bloated mass of it, would collapse. Water, sea – shit, wasn't everybody made of water? Didn't it come out of taps, didn't it puddle down in rancid pools in the council car parks? What was all this about a fucking stupid division, she would be thinking, between the water world and the land world? Weren't there brain-dead fishermen, kowtowing scuba divers, sailors with a venal sense of rising in the bitter and herpes-ridden hierarchy of sailors? But nothing she ever said worked. He turned everything she said around. He'd bought into this thing of water or boats and he wasn't going to let his mind-investment shrivel. Anything she said only fed into what he was saying all along: that there was this land-clogged world, and there was the freedom, the sublime existence, as he put it, of the ocean.

It seemed to her that all this talk was half making himself a beautiful obituary: this you have always thought I was shit and I always believed it myself, but now I am poetry, I am one of the golden people, I have found the meaning of things, I deserve to be remembered with reverence – half obituary and half weapon – I'll push you away with this poetry, you're not poetry, you stink. Or maybe, she thought, it was venal all along: he saw this boat in Newcastle or his old university mate had taken him along to a marina and showed him this boat, or else somebody he was jealous of (this mate or somebody else) had shown him their boat and he had suddenly become aware that the only thing that could remedy this terrible feeling in him, this stupid, fucking screwed-in-on-itself feeling, was to go and get a boat for himself and not only a boat that was just as good as his rival's, but a boat better than anything the other bugger would ever have been able to afford. You didn't work hard and stupidly for most of your adult life without some ounce of caring about dollars.

He'd had some money that Monique didn't know about and he could have spent it all on the family – a holiday somewhere, a shack in the mountains – fuck, she said, it would have been less hypocritical to spend it on a whore. Instead he ranted about the fucking ocean and accused her of triviality. He bought his boat because fortune smiled on him and he lost his job. All it took for men of this character was that moment when their lives or at least livelihoods were taken out of their own hands. That was all it took. Somebody, some institution acted; it didn't have to be a targeted action. A random act was enough, the random act of an institution. This random act or event was enough to make their moist little hot air bubble take shape. Her ex lost his job, got a payout, and the first thing he did was buy the boat he supposedly always wanted. Thus he covered this childish reaction of his with the rhetoric he no longer even believed in (or why would he prefer just to sit in that boat rather than cut gills in his neck and sink to the bottom of the ocean where he belonged?). He had the sea and freedom, he believed, and he simply no longer intended to provide for the rest of the family. Their sons at the private school could no longer go to the private school. She had to take them out of the private school and enrol them in a local school. It couldn't even be a selective school because it was too late to enrol them in a selective school. They had missed the relevant tests and the relevant cut-off dates for late submissions. Her ex didn't care. He'd bought his boat and, while he couldn't actually sail it himself, and nor did he know how to repair the 'ropes' nor where to buy new ones (he knew no more about them than she did, but at least she knew what a 'painter' was) he didn't know the first thing about boats, which was probably the very reason he felt so attracted to buying one in the first place. It didn't matter, he used to say, because he had a boat.

How very like a man, she said: he had a boat. So how the fuck could he complain when she spent up his fortnightly payments on this course they had all gone to? At least she'd had the nerve and the brains to say she didn't know about something and wanted to learn. Now she could work the shading so that a jug started to look like the three-dimensional object it was, but she was not going to fucking carve up the world between the creative and the not creative. She was learning something more. There was a whole lot of something out there and all those years she'd had to play the good wife and be the yes woman to her yes man, she hadn't known anything about it. Now it was up to her. She had to look around. She was keeping her head up now. She was going to look around her. Creativity was something concrete, she acknowledged: she was back onto the first definition but she didn't give a fuck. She wanted all of them to cut the shit and do something different.

The capitulation at the end of Monique's rant about creativity had been awkward, Trude said. It reminded her for some reason of her own decision to go on the workshop: of how she had given in to Murray's suggestion, and allowed him to pay for her to go. It was confusing for her, she told me, because the decision to go on the workshop and, in a sense, launch herself into the promise of an existence that she had never seriously entertained about herself before – the existence of someone who makes their art into their life – hadn't really been her own decision. She had given in to what Murray (and obviously our mother) had already decided for her. She'd made the best of the situation, and to an extent she'd got something out of it. She'd had a few days alone again (mostly) and had tested some of her nerve.

She hadn't got depressed about what she could do. It had been sort-of OK.

And yet, with the image of that door sliding shut in her head, sliding shut right in front of her without her being able to do anything about it, she knew she had to make a definite decision for herself. If she was ever to be an artist, she had to become one right then. There would be no going back to just playing at being an artist, or just thinking that she could be an artist if only the opportunity were there. There had been a break in her life, a decisive break. Sure, for once, she said, she could even see the accident on a larger scale: a much larger scale. The accident was a break, and her life had changed. She had moved in with Murray. She would never have met Murray if it hadn't been for the accident. All these years she had preferred living alone, and even after the accident she might have continued to do so, only she had been faced with that choice of either living with Murray or living with our parents.

All these months, she said, she had thought that the break in her life had been mostly about discovering a partner for her life. It had been a slow dawning, this realisation that she had been meant to meet Murray. In ordinary circumstances, she would never have let someone like Murray get any closer to her than from here to that door over there (she was pointing across at a door set back from a balcony in the building opposite us), much less allow herself to be involved with him in such a passive way. It was only by going against all her instincts, all her preferences, that she had found herself in the position which made it possible even to consider his proposition that she move in with him for a while.

All these months, then, it had been Murray who had concerned her. She had thought about herself only in relation to this other person who had changed her idea of herself and how she could live. All these years she had thought she had been made to live alone, when in reality – or so she had thought – she was no different to any other human being. She had thought she'd been meant to live alone when really that was an illusion that had been brought on by living more or less in the same kind of direction, never going against a single instinct or inborn prejudice. Our prejudices, or so she had thought until a few weeks ago, were made in the shape of our very tightest possibilities. The only way to get past this restriction on who we were, she said, was to go against our deepest instincts, to shut the doors of the heart and push on. This was how she had rationalised her relationship with Murray. She had certainly pushed against her feelings, although there had been other feelings too (it was never that simple, she admitted). But the most extraordinary thing was that she had instantly seen that she had been right to push forward in this way.

Very soon she had been happy that she had moved in with Murray – more than that, she had been thankful that at last she had the courage to take herself in her own hands and shake some sense into herself. There had been other things, she admitted, those other thoughts and associations, but it had been primarily that step of bravery which had shown her something new in herself: her capacity to live happily with somebody else. She couldn't discount this discovery. It was important in itself. In fact, she would go as far as saying that this discovery about other people and herself was the only way she could go further and see herself in another way yet again.

After thinking about the seemingly meaningless incident with the sliding door, she had found herself able to see herself in another way, and so it was only now that she realised that it all fitted together: that she had been meant to have the accident and, from that, for Murray to find her so that she might survive, her survival then making it possible for her to break first through the strictures of who she had been in order, or so she thought, that she could then become the artist she was meant to be. There was no other way she was going to be an artist than to have an accident smash a break through the life she had been living. She needed to have that accident, then, if being an artist was what she was in the innermost parts of her being, and so paradoxically, for her own survival, she had to have nearly died and have our mother intervene to send her on an art camp through the weak-strong new link who was Murray, her saviour in more ways than one.

She wanted to remind me of something that was crucial to this realisation. When she was just over two years old, which was well before I was born, our whole family had moved to Adelaide for a year, and it was the journey away from home that had made such an impression on her as to form the basis of a memory, a lasting memory.

In the vast night landscape outside of the train, the two-year-old Trude had seen a single, small house on a distant hill. The sky was dark but the house and the hill it was sitting on were darker. From two tiny windows, a thin yellow light was leaking out into the night. The house was far away and solitary. It looked empty and lonely despite, or perhaps because of, the thin yellowish light that was leaking out through its windows. The image must have only lasted a second on her retina and decades of billions of seconds had passed since then, and yet she still had that house on her retina, on the retina inside of her, its existence both magnified and infinitesimally reduced so that it was always tucked away in a place where it couldn't be lost.

All her life she had had this image inside her. It had simultaneously filled her with sadness to think of it and a longing for the solitude that had been promised by that house. While she was sitting in that room in the pub up north and had been seized by the conviction that she needed to be an artist, the image of that house in the darkness had come to her, and it was only then that she realised that the solitude and the longing and the beauty of the house was an image which represented the fact that she had always been destined to be an artist. Every now and then during her life, she said, she had tried to describe that view of the house on the hill that she had seen when she was two years old, but very few people ever believed her. She couldn't have been two, they'd say, she had to have been older. That nobody believed she could have a memory like that which dated back to when she was two was only further proof, she said, that she was meant to be an artist.

In a sense, all this time, all these decades which had passed since that moment, had already been stamped, as it were, with the meaning of being an artist, and the fact that she had simply not been aware of it said something about the terrible waste that had been her life thus far. It had taken an accident and Murray and an art workshop to begin to hack through the useless waste that had been her life until this moment. And while the accident and

Murray and the art workshop had each of them been significant, none of them by themselves had been strong enough to break through to the true meaning of the memory of the house on the hill. In combination, though, she said – the right kind of combination – they were plenty strong enough.

Despite the ridiculous poses and discussions at the art camp, there had been something in the accumulation of the moments of actual drawing, she told me, which coming hard on the heels of the accident and Murray, made it possible for that house on the hill to be found again. When you drew, she told me, you discovered what it was that you wanted to draw. Without the action of the drawing itself you couldn't find what it was. You didn't start with the drawing in your head and then make the lines emerge from the end of your pencil, their intersections all predetermined. All there was at the beginning (if you were lucky) was the instinct and the determination to draw something, despite feeling wholly unlike doing that activity at that moment. When the pencil hit the white, all there was was this instinct and this determination and then, if still lucky, just the scent of an image you pursued with your mind.

Had I ever, she asked me, had those dreams where you were speaking and every word you were saying came to you one at a time as if you were reading a script where nothing but one word at a time was ever visible? You said that word which you seemed to read from an invisible script, each word that came seeming to be able to connect (very surprisingly) to the word before it with the rhythm of inevitability, even grammatical sense, but never, as you spoke in the dream, did you seem to get the whole of what you were saying.

So it was with drawing, she said. There was always this pursuit, this instinct to move forwards. Afterwards, of course, there was the drawing itself, but at the time it felt to be nothing but chance that the drawing emerging, one line and then another, had any kind of cohesion, any kind of sense. Only later did you see it as a drawing. There was a moment near the end when you were glad you'd walked blind. Since the accident and Murray and then the drawings at the art camp, she said, everything had this extra meaning, although without the train of thoughts that came after the incident with the door it all might have just seeped away slowly, and soon there would only have been Murray again and in a few months, work, and then nothing much after that. Nothing in particular.

All of this, of course, went through her mind much quicker than she could now tell me. It went through her mind in a second – perhaps less than a second – and so at the end of it, there was still that awkward conclusion of Monique's rant, an awkwardness that got to her, until she realised that, as with the sliding door and the memory of the house, there was an inescapable thingness about what was in front of her: in this case the particular arrangement of features on Monique's face – a pleating of flesh around a mouth and the nose, a slight shaking in the jaw line – an arrangement of features she now wanted to capture.

She tried drawing with a wet forefinger on the table (like Toulouse Lautrec had done in Paris, she'd thought, although she didn't know whether this anecdote was in fact true). This crude gesture concentrated the most basic lines of the arrangement of features she wanted to capture: the pleating of flesh, the indeterminate jaw. An artist is always an artist, she was beginning to realise, and so every waking moment has to be a creating moment. She could be Cézanne seeing the sublimely simple in the complexity of ordinary forms. In Monique, she said, she saw an inverted letter Y with a couple of dark lines over its head like a Japanese yen sign slipped beneath its hatches and fallen upside down.

In drawing it on the table, she drew attention to herself. William wanted to know what she was doing. Monique, inevitably, wanted to know too. For the first time, people began to notice her, Trude said, and it was only as a result of this intrusion of drawing (however invisible). Monique began to describe to the others about how well Trude had drawn people at the workshop. Trude could really draw people, she was saying. They should have seen how she did the models, and even on the first day (before they had had the session with the manikin). One line here, one line there. Monique said she would have fucking given anything to draw the models like Trude did. She drew so well it made Monique want to puke. And yet these days, she had to admit, who gave a shit about how well people drew? What was drawing but weaving a fucking basket? What use did they have for hand-woven baskets when they could get cheaper-than-shit baskets in Campsie or Lakemba? Monique knew they had to practise drawing at the workshop but the whole time they were there the teachers had told them that drawing wasn't everything. Only art was that everything, they were told. They had to release what was inside them and create goddamn fabulous works of art. And now she had learned a whole lot more about it, Monique was saying, she wanted to create art, not just mimic a fucking camera – and yet, the fuck of the thing was that this Trude woman was the only bloody person at the camp who could make you feel sad looking at a body or feel shitty, whatever. New definition of that so-called creativity, Monique then posed: this thing that caused you to feel like shit?

It was only then, said Trude, she realised that all the time when she had drawn at the workshop, seemingly unnoticed and unpraised, someone else had been noticing what she was doing. How she had longed all that time at the workshop for someone to mention how well she could draw as they used to do when she was at school. Wasn't that the main reason, she thought then, that she had come – that it had been a trial of a sort – and more than discovering that she could still draw, that joy of discovering that someone might talk about it, that she might be characterised as someone who could draw well and could therefore have a hold on other people in a way that no other person could have a hold on other people, no matter what they did or how hard they tried?

William then leaned over the table where she had been drawing, saying somebody for god's sake should get her some paper as he didn't want her ruining his tables, so Trude said she decided to go the whole hog. She opened her small backpack to get the pad of cartridge paper she had brought along for the workshop and had been carrying around with her the whole time. She took a thinnish stick of charcoal from a box lined with tissues. Ordinarily, she told me, she wouldn't have done such a thing. Not since she was at high school would she have thus shown off and certainly not in front of some of the people who had been with her at the workshop, some of the people from there as well as William.

Monique had then challenged William. She thought the hotel wasn't his and so neither should the tables have been. If the hotel didn't belong to him, he couldn't exactly call them his tables. It was a small exchange and an apparently meaningless one, but the way William leaned over as he questioned whether he had really said the tables had been his – the way he subsequently leaned over further to take the last sausage from the plate in the middle of the table (then held it between his thumb and middle finger, sniffing it, before putting it back on the plate) – the way William had enacted all these gestures made Trude decide that she would draw William instead of Monique. Drawing gave you power. Once you were given permission just to draw, you didn't need to do anything else. When you drew someone, you became them and through that became something slightly different to everyone else. It was a way of cutting loose, she thought, a freedom both to be ignored (as something other) and superficially admired.

As soon as she started, it was obvious that William was very aware he was being drawn. He sat down and leaned back in his chair. He tilted his face very slightly upwards, and at an angle that suggested he had already decided to preclude a view of his right ear (whose lobe, she had noticed before, was twisted by a scar). It made her want to laugh at this careful positioning of his person for her. Since she had already seen the scar, she could very easily have put it in anyway because did I remember, she now asked me, how she used to do the primary school fetes, drawing pictures of kids so that she could help raise money for our school? Did I use to notice how the mothers would all get out their combs to smooth the hair of their children before they were sat down for Trude to draw them? Had I remembered how the mothers would straighten their children's necklines or pull out the bows in their hair so that they stood out very neatly? It was ridiculous, she said, because they didn't seem to understand that she wasn't a camera. She could do their child's hair or neckline in any way she liked. She could even make the child's nose bigger or straighter, the teeth slightly protruding. It was touching, those little efforts the mothers made. It was the first time that she realised the power you had when you sat down and drew someone.

At the workshop, she said, the models were just the other tutors and none of them seemed to care too much whether they were hung this way or that way, let alone the way their hair fell. Of course they were artists themselves, so they didn't have any illusions. It wasn't until she started drawing William that she remembered what she could do.

William evidently liked being drawn but she could see he was restless. He said he wanted to be entertained. There was nothing more fucking boring than being drawn, he said (as if it had happened to him a hundred times before). Monique had already entertained them with the story of her loser ex-husband and how she had come to enrol herself in the art camp up the river – a story, he said, which told us very little about Monique and too much about fish – but he wanted to hear some other explanations. They could charge their glasses, he said, and go get drinks from the main bar. Drinks were all the better if they kept people talking, and they could tell Dave if he was there that this round was on William. But no one was to go upstairs before they had fully explained themselves, and they had better believe him if they didn't want enacted the very direst consequences they could possibly imagine: a threat, Trude said, which had the effect he must have envisaged, because everyone but herself, the fat man (and of course William) shifted themselves off to the main bar to get a drink before settling themselves down in this smaller room again.

Trude said that she had already thought about such things – for weeks and weeks since Murray had first raised the issue, she had been thinking about little else other than why it was she had allowed herself to be persuaded to go to the Getaway Art Workshop, as I knew. But although she had spent weeks by herself trying to get to the bottom of the same question, she thought that she had no interest whatsoever in hearing the same kind of analysis from anybody else. While the question had involved her for weeks and weeks – and in fact was still involving her – the moment when William had suggested they all fully explain themselves, it was the last thing she felt like listening to. If it had been possible, she said, she might have left the room or at least stopped her ears with her hands. But it was impossible to either leave the room or stop her ears with her hands while she was drawing William and, while she had no interest in hearing the others fully explain themselves, she also knew that if she stopped drawing William and left the room to go back upstairs, this small thing that was at last beginning to develop out of herself – this decision to make the effort to become an artist at last – all this would have to stop.

In fact, in the end, while she'd thought she would have no interest in what the others had to say, the moment that they all began to explain themselves as they had been instructed, she couldn't help but be drawn in. That their reasons for enrolling were completely different from her own – so different that it surprised her that anybody could be so compelled by what seemed such spurious and superficial and even frivolous reasons for spending so much money and a good few days on what now struck her as a piece of clever marketing on the part of a few artists or art teachers – all this did not in itself diminish the interest she had in what they began to say. The fact that they were sufficient to make the person (each of her fellow art workshop students) stick their neck out as the saying goes by allowing themselves to be exploited so cleverly by a few market-savvy artists or art teachers on the upper north coast of New South Wales – this in itself was fascinating. She was embarrassed on their behalf (as she also realised that she was embarrassed on her own behalf), but she noticed that her fellow art workshop students were not embarrassed whatsoever. The ultimate offering that the workshop had held out to them – the promise of becoming an artist through the sheer exercise of filling in a credit card form online and then following the instructions – was obviously enough to mask the supremely humiliating position that they had all got themselves into by enrolling in the Getaway Art Workshop on the north coast of New South Wales. It was as if each of them were so eager to be called an 'artist' that they would do anything, even buy the privilege online and then abase themselves by pretending to swallow the exotic art workshop location bullshit during a workshop in which nothing was actually different from any other art work-shop they might have gone on.

Monique, as it happened, wanted to be the first to talk. Although she had already talked before, she was eager to say more. She wanted to explain herself by extending her discussion, as she put it, of the gullibility of her ex. She was offended that all William had remembered about what she'd had to say was the little she'd said about fish. What she had said about the gullibility of her ex was relevant to what William was wanting them all to describe now.

If they didn't believe what she said about the gullibility of her husband, they needed to hear what happened to a friend of hers who based all the moves in her life on a couple of chance encounters with a couple of people. This friend of hers, whom she called Sally (in case we knew her) on account of her blonde hair, this friend was born in the States, up near the Canadian border, and grew up in one of those large, distracted families, where none of the children felt they ever got the attention of their parents and there-fore later had to head off at the deep end in an attempt to find it. One of her brothers took to shoplifting big time and landed himself in a juvenile detention centre where he learned all the basics of car stealing and karate. This gave him a good fifteen-year career both in and out of jail before a conversion to Jesus Christ set him hot on a money-lending business in Iowa.

That was just the brother, Monique said. All of them went their ways, one way or another, and Sally, she took it into her head to get as far away from her family as she could. That was back in the days of *Crocodile Dundee* movies. One afternoon, after seeing the second movie with one of her friends at the cinema, this Sally had seen the same Paul Hogan sitting over in a bar down the street not two hours after the show. He was very unlike the way he had appeared in the movie, she told Monique later. For one thing, his teeth didn't seem so white nor his skin so brown. But she knew, from the very first sighting of him in that bar, that he wasn't sitting in that bar across from where she was sitting for nothing. Her hair, after all, had been as blonde as the heroine's. There was no reason for not being a heroine herself. So she bought herself a return ticket to Australia just to have a see and, after a few months of soaking up the sunshine during one of our protracted droughts, she threw away the return ticket and organised for herself to stay.

In Australia she did one course after another. She was a junkie for courses – mostly those naturopathic kinds of courses – but with her accent and her hair (which she had taken to piling up in a retro beehive), no one ever expected anything different from her. Monique said she knew her very slightly when she was going along to the same yoga class. They both were of a larger build and found the classes, as they admitted to each other, both tiring and embarrassing. They would occasionally have a coffee afterwards; sometimes just the two of them, sometimes a few others too.

But then Monique didn't see her for some years. It was after she and her ex had already split, when Monique decided to take a trip without the kids to visit some friends in the UK and who else should she see in a café in London but the very same Sally who, years ago, she used to have coffee with after yoga. Sally had changed quite a lot. Perhaps she'd changed too, Monique thought – changes in relationships can do that. Instead of being big, Sally was now thin – very thin – and very brown and had dyed her hair red. She had discovered art too – in fact, that was why she was over there in London. She'd enrolled herself in this course on the east side. It had come to her several years ago, when she'd gone along to an exhibition of London artists in Canberra. She could be an artist, she'd decided, so she'd squeezed back on her hours at the Healthy Life Alternative (where she'd been working for some years as both a masseuse and iridologist) and enrolled herself in a full-time art class in Sydney. But London was the place to be, she soon discovered. She had read about it in a magazine (and there was that first exhibition of course too, all those images of the Tate). It was her little treat. So she had sent herself to London for a course.

Funny thing was that the very day Monique arrived back in Sydney – she'd caught a taxi straight home, but it was too early to wake the kids and her sister who'd been looking after them – she went out to this local café and who should be there but that woman Sally again. They were amazed to see each other, and so soon after meeting up in London. It was a sign, Sally kept telling Monique. It was definitely a sign. After that, she would ring Monique. It would sometimes be late at night. Could Monique help her at that very moment, Sally would ask, because she needed someone with a car who could move a few canvases over to her studio in Newtown? Monique would be alone with the kids and there was always something she was in the middle of (a crisis, for example, with one of the boys), so Monique would have to say no, she was sorry – unless Sally could wait until the weekend (which she couldn't). There were a couple of similar requests, which for one reason or another she'd been unable to meet.

The last time Monique ever heard from her was a long message she left on Monique's answering machine. Sally was moving to Korea, she told the machine, because she'd got a job over there. It was a teaching job and she was only sorry it had taken her this long in her life to discover that teaching was the only means of discovering a direct communication with people. Korea was a long way away, but at least it offered her a three-year contract. In fact, she was glad she'd got a job over there, far from everyone here who had only ever let her down one way and another. She had forgiven Monique, she said, and she never wanted to talk about it again, but Monique had been selfish and heartless at the very time in her life when she had most needed her. Monique was a cruel and hurtful person. She had only ever talked about herself and her ruined relationship and the children who nauseated her. Sally had been struggling for years just to be the artist she knew she had it in her to be, but without support from her friends she'd been able to do nothing.

Monique said that she never knew Sally very well, but after that message she'd felt her inner world collapsing. Right through the break-up with her ex, she had held her own and made decisions that would help her get back on her feet so she could be the kind of mother, she felt, that wouldn't drag her children down. She couldn't help but think that Sally was entirely right in her judgement of her – that Monique was in fact a selfish and heartless person – and that there was nothing in anything she did but a kind of petty going round and around all the tasks that had to be done in one day, in one week.

Monique talked about it to a friend of hers the next day. She asked the friend, do you think I am selfish and inflexible? Am I letting everything important pass by me in my life? The friend of Monique had then said what she expected her to say – why else would she have asked a friend (a good friend)? – that Monique was not selfish, not at all; in fact, she was the most selfless person she had ever known, and as for inflexibility, it was blah, blah, blah.

Monique enjoyed believing her friend as she talked. She also told her friend about Sally and her incurable tendency to make drastic changes in her life. It was easy to laugh at Sally and to feel entirely in the right. All the same, while Monique and her friend were sitting there, Monique had the definite conviction – a conviction that grew for some time after that conversation – that all she ever did with her friends was to lie to them kindly, and in fact that was what they wanted and what she wanted too. They were only her friends, Monique realised, because they lied to her and she lied to them in the way they had all tacitly agreed to lie. There was no way, then, that her friend was ever going to tell her what was true about herself – at least not intentionally – and so all she had, then, was Sally and her obsession with her own destiny, which gave a particular distortion to her way of looking at other people, and which, although nonetheless a distortion, could have been as true if not more true than anything one of Monique's real friends might have told her. And so for a time, Monique said, she felt very down about herself. She had never felt as down about herself as she did after Sally's message (and particularly after her conversation with her reassuring friend).

And then one day, on her way to work after dropping off the kids at the station, it came to her that, if she was such a selfish person, there was no reason why she mightn't be an artist like Sally was. In one sense, becoming an artist would be going the whole hog and being the most selfish and, in a sense, inflexible (at least with regards to her interests) person that she could possibly be. For a long time it had been just a consoling thought, but these days, Monique said, she was getting out there more. She was tougher than she was even two years ago, which was before the message from Sally. She was getting older – older and older every day – and come fifty, she had decided, she didn't want her life to be recognisable to someone like Sally who might bump into her again in a café in some godforsaken bit of earth – who knows, Monique then said, she could be in this pub, right here – back to naturopathy or pyramid selling, or gone on to palm reading. That was more Sally's style, she said – the reading of the arbitrary lines and bumps on their bodies. Sally had always been one of those gullible types, the types that go colliding with people, who send all sorts of things flying as they swallow the one thing they have in their mouths for the moment. But she did Monique a favour, this Sally, because without her Monique wouldn't be here in this pub feeling refreshed and inspired after a couple of days of learning about art. God only knew where she would have been. Monique was meant to know Sally, fucking barmy as she was. All this seemed so obvious now, she said.

Jay was the next to speak, said Trude. She said it was interesting that Monique had talked about things that were meant to happen. Jay didn't want to talk about herself particularly, because it went without saying that she had always been interested in drawing and painting, and these days she needed to do something now and then – finance a kick in the bum, so to speak – just to keep her interest going, so that it might not be swamped by her other life as a case worker. But speaking of signs, she said, when her mother died, she had suddenly got the feeling that she hadn't much time in the world herself: an irrational thought, but all the same it got her thinking. And then one day she had woken up with the number forty-eight on her lips. She didn't know what it meant. Even at the time of waking she had already forgotten the dream it must have come from. It could have meant anything. But on the train that day, she had been overcome by the conviction that the number referred to the age at which she was going to die. It was not all that long in the future, because she was already thirty-four. That meant, she said, that she would only have fourteen years left to live. And yet, even as she calculated this – without wanting to – she also knew that there was no reason why she should draw this conclusion. The number might have meant anything, and even if it meant something like the price of something, or the number of girlfriends she was ever going to have, all the same, she said, it was only a dream. Every day we dream of things that don't happen or couldn't happen.

Once, she'd had a dream of having teeth in a band all around the outside of her face. Patently this had nothing to do with reality. She only had the teeth we all had which were inside her mouth, and so, following on from this, she knew that it was ridiculous to suppose that she might die at the age of forty-eight on the strength of a dream or the aftermath of a dream. And yet this could not be proved until she had already reached the age of forty-nine, which was even longer – fifteen years away. And so, to distract herself, and also to hedge her bets, she had decided then to live as if the age of forty-eight was her deadline, so to speak.

This was why she had decided to send herself on some more serious art courses. At first she hadn't enjoyed them, and had only felt useless. In one course, all the teacher had been obsessed with was what she had called 'a clarity of palette'. It was then, during the frustration of that class, that she realised that she had never been interested in colour, which made her begin to feel herself a fraud for even thinking of going to an art class at all. There were all sorts of things about art (like colour and line) that she really wasn't interested in, and this made it all the more stupid that she should want to spend any of her precious time doing classes which forced her to think about either colour or line (or both). Either she was naturally perverse, she said, or she simply had no feeling for those aspects of a picture. All in all, she didn't know why she had spent so much time and also money on all the courses she had done, but there was still that residue of thinking that she was doing the right thing in the face of the knowledge that she would die at the age of forty-eight.

Grace now said she would tell them a story. Hers was just something she had read somewhere, although it still related to why she had gone on the art camp, she assured William. This woman, she said, had left her country and gone to the northern hemisphere to live (it was either Europe or northern America, she couldn't remember which). She'd decided that the only way to become the person she had always wanted to was by living somewhere else, right away from her family and friends, away from everything that had surrounded her when she was young. She'd grown up in what some might say were ideal surroundings: one of those old but outer suburbs that are close to bushland, where magpies and currawongs, noisy mynas and koels thread the clear, crisp air with their various calls. All this, however, was lost on the young woman who, to the despair of her parents, seemed to prefer the squalor of student living far from the suburban home, in inner city suburbs which were notorious for their filth and crime.

When she announced her intention to go travelling to the northern hemisphere (as did many of her age after they had finished their studies), her parents were glad to support her. Travel would broaden her mind, her parents knew, and it would only be when their daughter was far away from home and surrounded, as they hoped, by the beauties of more cultured countries than their own, that she would finally come to appreciate the decisions they had made on behalf of their family by choosing to live in a leafy and reputable suburb very far away from the filth and crime of other places.

Their daughter left the country, then, with what she believed to be their blessing. Fairly soon she got to making her life far from them, and in relation to nobody but herself. At first the life she made had seemed provisional. All the opportunities that came her way were only variously interesting, and whatever she did – whether it was teaching or working in a bar – seemed to her to be only the response to the moment and so not yet the destiny which she had dreamed to be hers the moment she could cut herself free from the fetters, as she'd put it, of her family and childhood friends.

After some years had passed, the arbitrariness of her circumstances began to get to her. She was living in a temperate coastal city at the time, which both reminded and didn't remind her of the city (Sydney) she had left. She had never been particularly interested in the usual attractions of coastal life – the surf, the sunbaking, the cafés on the sand – and so it seemed strange to her that she should find herself living in such a city when she had always imagined herself somewhere more remote and much colder. There was no reason why she shouldn't move somewhere like that, she used to tell herself, but there was also no reason, she found, to send herself somewhere else yet again, to a city she didn't know.

It was then that she began to think back to the life she had led in Australia, where her dreams of becoming something special – something in particular and not the arbitrarily assembled kind of person she felt herself to be now – where her dreams of becoming something special had at least been very real and certainly possible. There must have been something about her life in that leafy outer suburb of Sydney, something about her family and her childhood friends, which had at least given her a coherent sense of who she was, a sufficiently coherent sense of where she was in the world (a position, if only that, from which to depart). And so she became nostalgic for the very same people and places she had been in a hurry to escape from more than a decade in the past.

In the end, said Grace, this woman came back to Sydney, and of course never found what it was that she was looking for. All certainties about herself and what she had dreamed of as a child had entirely disappeared. Grace had a feeling, now she was finishing the story, that she had actually heard the gist of this tale in a lecture, or perhaps one of those interview programs on the radio, in which case the woman had either gone on to write a novel about it or had actually done something someone had wanted to ask her about after all, because otherwise there would have been no reason for anyone to have asked her to speak about so vague an experience.

She herself, said Grace, found she was very critical of this woman who had spent so much of her life not knowing precisely enough what it was she wanted to do. This woman had had all these experiences, she said, but had done absolutely nothing with them – at least nothing worth remembering. Grace said she herself wouldn't be able to stand leading so meaningless and indecisive an existence, which was why she had actually decided to borrow the money she needed to send herself on the art camp they had gone to.

It had been a fantastic experience and she had learned such a lot. She was very happy she was someone who did things, rather than someone who only talked about it but in fact did nothing at all.

Trude said that everyone had quite liked Grace's story about the woman who had lost her direction in life, which had surprised her, since it seemed fairly pointless. What she suspected people liked best was the bit of moralising at the end. All in all, she said, everyone was convinced that they had done the right thing by going out of their way for this one experience for themselves – this Getaway Art Workshop up the coast. Even William who, during Jay's short tale, had looked restless and bored, had seemed to sit still during this story of almost nothing, and even smile as he stared past her towards the open door that led to the main bar.

Just to stop him drifting off altogether, which he might well have done, Trude said that she decided to tell everyone there about the friend of hers from school whose brother had disappeared. This had happened a long time ago, when we were all still at school. This friend of hers came from a large family – several brothers and several sisters – which was as unusual as our large family of girls. The family had always seemed quite an ordinary family otherwise. The father went out to work and, as often was the way then, the mother stayed at home. Perhaps since they were such a big family, as with ours, the children never got any new clothes of their own. All the clothes were hand-me-downs, either from one set of cousins who lived out near Dubbo, or another, much older set who lived in Melbourne (and who often handed their clothes down through the Dubbo family before they ever came to the family in Sydney). Again, this wasn't unusual, considering how many of them there were, and how expensive it would have been to clothe them all otherwise.

The mother was very anxious about her children's future. Unless they were all to grow up and become professionals, she would say, they would face even greater difficulties than their parents had had to face, considering, at least, that the bulk of the down payment for their house had come from their grandfather's will, which had only been split three times, while theirs would be split many, many times and so would be worth virtually nothing (and even so, would not benefit any of them for some time to come). These children, of course, were all children of the 'seventies, and so could not even begin to imagine life – their future – as their mother had described it. While they did feel themselves to be deprived in some ways, they all lived in a big house and a relatively safe and secure suburb, so their comparative poverty didn't hurt them as much as it seemed to hurt their mother.

For all her anxieties, Trude said, this mother was not an overly directive kind of mother, and so the children had a fabulous time running around their garden and the many rooms of their house, being independent of their mother who, for her sanity, had taken up china doll painting in a remote corner of the house. With their freedom and comparative neglect, many of them began to develop ideas of doing something extraordinary with their lives: one, who had unusual flexibility, dreamed of becoming an Olympic gold medal gymnast or a circus acrobat; another wanted to be a famous singer (as good as Olivia Newton-John); one wanted to do drag racing; another to be a poet. But the moment any of these children ever breathed a word of their dreams to their mother, this mother, instead of smiling and indulging these childish fantasies, would become fearful of what her child was saying and not only begin actively to discourage them from any activity that might lead to such an outcome (by proffering numerous arguments about why such and such career was either dangerous, ludicrous, precarious or all three), but would also seek – and here their mother was most successful – to try and implant more so-called wholesome and practical ideas about how the children should prepare for their future.

All this, of course, said Trude, had the very opposite effect on them to the one that the mother had been hoping for. Instead of succeeding in turning her daughter off the circus through her many second-hand tales of broken legs, broken backs, rotten teeth and bad taste in jewellery, all she succeeded in doing was to make her daughter even more attached to the idea of the circus ring than ever. This particular daughter, the mother had always said, would make a good doctor – and the family (as all families) could very well do with a doctor. The thing was to become the doctor first, said the mother and, when she was firmly enough established in her career, to pursue her interest in contorting herself in her own time. Degrees at university would not always be free, the mother would wisely counsel. She would be a fool not to take up the opportunity that was staring her in the face. This girl was only fourteen at the time, Trude said, but already, through this conflict, had become unusually attached to her idea of developing into a world-famous gymnast or at least an extraordinary trapeze artist, so that all her spare time away from the now prying eyes of her mother was taken up with practising continually and determinedly all the moves she had learned at the local YWCA gym class from which her mother had now banned her.

Much the same happened, said Trude, with almost all of the other children. Their mother who had until then seemed quite happy that they entertained themselves in the large house she and her husband had provided for them, now spent the greater part of her time devising ways to steer her children away from the obsessions they had developed and trying to interest them in what she saw as more suitable pursuits such as language learning, classical music and chess. With one or two of her children, these new interests had in fact taken root but it was not long before even these more sober and productive interests had become obsessions. There was no getting away from the matter, she would tell any other parents who would listen: her children had all got their obsessional gene from her husband, whom she now accused of being too interested in his work and too little interested in the lives of his various children (some of whose names he couldn't even pronounce correctly – as with the gymnast who was called Charmian and whom he invariably called 'Charmin').

One of the children, though, seemed less obsessed than the others, and while this might have cheered the mother, it in fact worried her dreadfully. All the time that this boy's siblings had been pursuing this or that dream in the wide freedom of their largely unsupervised house, he had only ever wanted to get out of the house and see other friends of his somewhere else. This particular boy was not noticeably athletic or flexible. He was neither interested in chess nor poetry nor drag racing. There might have been something that he was good at, Trude said, but his sisters and brothers never told her anything about it. Perhaps they were all too busy with their own private wars with their mother to notice. As this particular brother got older, he would be prone to sudden, inexplicable outbursts of violence. Once, in a fit of temper, he stabbed the wooden kitchen table so hard that the blade of the knife he was using snapped clean in half. Another time, she was told, he broke a window with his fist and had to go to hospital to get eleven stitches in his hand, the black threads wiring his knuckles like newly grown, monstrous hairs. The father of the family, now brought under pressure from the seeming irrationality of his son, would himself begin to fly into rages more frightening than the boy's.

Then one evening at dinner, after an unusually quiet main course, during which the son had hissed something irritably at one of his sisters and had received a reply more irrational than insulting, their father had stood up and, with his eyes closed in frustration and despair, shouted at his son to get out of the house. The son had said something (no one could remember what it was exactly to this day) and, without looking at anybody in particular – in fact avoiding the eyes of everybody who was watching – he ran out of the cold, empty family room and into the dark of the garden. He was sixteen at the time, perhaps sixteen and a half. He must have changed his name or something, unless he had succeeded in killing himself very cleverly (that is, disposing of his body at the same moment he had disposed of his life) because it had been more than twenty years since he had left and the police had never been able to find any trace of him.

There was a silence in the room when Trude had finished this part of the story. It was the silence, she said, of people who had heard a story reach a satisfying conclusion. Nevertheless, she had decided to continue with the aftermath of the boy's departure. After that, she told them, there were still the usual arguments with the mother. After a short time of grieving and blaming (mostly blaming, although there were the frequent tearful nights), the mother had assembled them all one evening after dinner, even standing in the way of the television so that she might grab their attention for a while. It was terrible about the son who had left them, she'd declared. He was a stupid fool if he thought that at sixteen he knew enough to get along in the world without a whisper of guidance from anyone. The only people who cared anything for her children were in fact herself and their father. They alone knew what was best for their children. They alone put them first. The least they could all do, she then said, was to listen to her, just to listen to her for once. God knew she had suffered enough as it was.

In the end, as it turned out, the mother got her various professionals. The son who had wanted to do drag racing gave in to pressure to do an accounting degree, and now lived in London. The one who'd got particularly into chess was now a public relations manager. The gymnast became a doctor and had recently got her exam in paediatrics even though she had never liked children.

The one who had been her friend, Trude said, was the one who had wanted to be a poet. This girl went through a rough patch after her brother disappeared – she was anorexic for some years – but these days she worked as a general library assistant at a council library, perhaps the least well paying of all the children's careers. This ex-poet didn't like her work at the library, but couldn't imagine doing anything else. At one time, she'd had an obsession with trying to find her brother and through her contacts at other libraries she searched government databases for any information that might connect her to the brother she had lost. While no information had ever come to light, there were several times, apparently, when she was sure she had seen him. The last time Trude spoke with the ex-poet, the now-librarian had even referred very casually to the fact that she had seen her long-lost brother only the other day on Market Street in the city, and that he had told her that he was out looking for an outfit for a wedding (but she hadn't thought to ask whose wedding it was for until afterwards). It went without saying, Trude had then said, that it was commonly understood that this sister the librarian was thought to be a sad case by her brothers and sisters. They said she was continually inventing nonsensical encounters with the brother they had all lost. Each time, they said, her accounts of meeting their brother became more and more impossible to believe.

She hadn't exactly intended it, Trude said, but this little extension of the story had very obviously depressed the others in the room behind the bar. At the end of it William got up, as if he had suddenly forgotten that someone was drawing him (which was understandable, as Trude had stopped work on the drawing halfway through the telling of her story), and he began to walk back and forth in the room, cracking the joints in his fingers and shaking his head.

He couldn't stand hearing about people like that, William said. People like that were totally depressing (meaning people like the librarian, very evidently, Trude thought). He and Dave had a sister like that. She too was a fairly hopeless kind of person, but he wouldn't say exactly what she was doing now in case any of them happened to know her. An example of what she was like should be obvious, he said, from this story she had only recently told him the last time she had come to Singapore to visit him. Now that he was in Australia on this family holiday leave, he had thought of visiting this sister and his other much younger sister who lived in Hobart, but he didn't particularly feel like doing either of those things for the moment. Right now, he said, hanging out at this half pub with his wacko older *frère* was sufficiently amusing and at least a bit relaxing. One wacko sibling at a time was all he could cope with.

When this particular sister had visited him, she had only recently left a relationship that she'd been in for many years. This she didn't tell him straight away but, as was her wont, meandered around the subject, dropping little comments about his own relationship with his boyfriend that might have been an invitation for him to ask her questions in reply. This sister had always had an indirect way about her. Even as a kid she had got on his wick for never getting out a single straight observation about anything. The story she told him, however, was noticeable for its frankness, and so for this reason alone he'd had grave doubts as to how true it was and therefore what planet she'd been living on all this while.

Several months ago, this sister had had a dream. She had already forgotten the setting of the dream, but she still had a sense of one of those huge old hotels she had seen in BBC telemovies – the sort with rambling gardens and empty wicker chairs under rose-covered trellises and so forth – the kind of place where the few guests rattle around in the lethargy of cavernous dining rooms and eventually meet up in one of the sitting rooms after supper, where they come to realise that they had all known each other at one time or other in their pasts.

In this dream, his sister eventually recognised a boy with whom she had been to high school. Over the years, she told William, she had often seen this boy in her dreams. In her recent dream, though, he did something unusual because he expressed his still supposedly ardent desire for her – in smiles and gestures, it seems; no words were exchanged – and she was sorely torn (even in the dream) about what to do about this wordless declaration.

In the dream, as it turned out, William's sister had just married a very colourfully dressed and kindly older man from a country in South America. The moment she thought about her husband he seemed also to be there in the hotel with her but only in the form of a mute and supplicatory figure. Also in the dream, as it happened, was her younger sister, and the older sister had then turned to this younger sister to whom she had not even talked in reality for years, just to ask for advice as to what to do about her situation. Should she tell her husband there had been a terrible misunderstanding? Should she tell him that all this time the boy from her high school had desired her and she desired him? Her sister had advised not telling her husband anything. Just stay married, the younger sister had told her, and see the high school boy now and then when it suited.

The strangest thing about this dream was not the dream itself, apparently. William's sister had dreamed about this boy every couple of years or so since she had left school. When she woke up out of the dream, it was just after five in the morning and her house was very quiet. She lay thinking about the dream: about the inevitability of seeing the boy in her dreams again and about the pathos of the husband figure, who was not in fact her husband at all, but just an image of the mutely innocent other figure in this dream scenario with the boy. The husband figure in the dream was an older man, but as she thought about it she realised that it was strange that, in her dream, the boy from her high school should not have aged as she had – that he was still a boy – and although her dream-age was indeterminate, she was well and truly a grown adult. And yet the desire between them had been a desire of contemporaries, as if at the same time she was both an experienced adult and a fresh-faced teenager.

When she thought about this anomaly of ages, she also remembered one of her school friends mentioning that she had seen this same boy several years earlier. They had both been waiting at the same supermarket check-out queue in Chatswood. The friend recognised him immediately but also noticed how much he had aged. He looked just like any other middle-aged man in the supermarket, the friend had said. William's sister then wondered whether trying to think of this boy as a middle-aged man might have the effect of ridding her of the recurring nuisance of his presence in her dreams – these dreams which always ended with her waking into a helpless longing and dissatisfaction with her life.

She then thought back to her last years at high school. She had always been attracted to him, she realised, but in year eleven the boy had gone away. Then, during the holidays between year eleven and twelve, she had been involved in a small choir which had gone from nursing home to nursing home singing Christmas carols and other festive songs. It was at a party after one such occasion when one of the choristers had asked her whether she wanted to go out with him and, flattered that anyone should find her attractive at all, William's sister had said 'yes'. This chorister had come from a wealthy background and liked throwing parties at his house, but such was her inexperience and her lack of confidence in herself that she never once wondered why he didn't want to touch her or kiss her or she want to touch or kiss him. She was his girlfriend, supposedly, and that was enough for her. In fact, if he had wanted to touch her, she thought afterwards, she would have been instantly horrified. This boyfriend was a strange individual – highly narcissistic and obsessed by a supposed career he thought was his (by right of privilege and so-called talent) on the opera stage – but all the same she was his girlfriend, she had thought then, because she had said the word 'yes'.

When school returned for year twelve, William's sister saw that the other boy had returned. Immediately among her circle of friends, this boy was included in their childish list of who loved whom and who wanted to be married to whom. One of her friends loved this boy and was always talking about him. She wanted to get married to him and would talk of the children they would have. And then one day this boy had asked William's sister out to a family event. Nothing could have been more confusing for her. To this day, she didn't know what she said first: either that she already had a boyfriend or that her friend was the one who liked him (and therefore, by implication, for her to accept would have been morally wrong). All the time, however, she regretted what she thought she had to say to him. She wished she could have said 'yes' to his invitation. Not long afterwards, she ceased – to her relief – being girlfriend to the opera star pretender. At last she was free, she then thought, and the boy should ask her out again. But he never did.

Like the girl in Trude's story, said William, his sister went through years of eating disorders. It was very boring. The whole family became obsessed with it and were always asking themselves why the problem of eating disorders had struck their family. Now and then his sister aired to him some of her views about the disorders she had since left behind. At one time she blamed her mother, at another a confused relationship she'd had while at university. She now, though (or so she told him in Singapore), had a very different perspective on the whole thing, and this idea had occurred to her in the first cold moments after she had awakened from her most recent dream about the high school boy. Why was it that, despite the abject pitifulness of the opera singer boyfriend – the uselessness of their supposed relationship – and the girl-sealed finality of her friend's apparent determination to marry the boy one day – that she hadn't been forthright enough in declaring what she knew to be right: that she had wanted to go out with this boy and she should have said 'yes' to him? What had been the honour she had upheld over the boyfriend who had never even once said that he cared for her and between whom there had never been any attraction, only repugnance? How would her friend's declaration of love for this boy have any relevance to him or even to her? Why hadn't she said how much she wanted to agree to his offer, even if she had still felt it necessary to refuse for the moment? And even given that she didn't agree at the time, why didn't she feel able to initiate anything with him afterwards, when the boyfriend had vanished and she no longer felt so compelled to honour her friend's preferences?

For the first time, William's sister said, she realised that this awkward moment between them might have affected the boy as much as it had affected her. Perhaps he had been marked for life by the strangeness of her response, and become a tired, cynical middle-aged man – the man her friend had seen in the supermarket in Chatswood. And yet, for all this, she didn't think she had any illusions about what the relationship between them might have been like had they successfully got together. They would have had little in common, and their relationship as teenagers probably wouldn't have lasted more than a year.

The thought that her combined lack of generosity, honesty and bravery in refusing the boy might have affected him as much as it had evidently (or so she had decided) affected her, led to her being in a preoccupied state for a number of weeks, she told William. And although the mute and pathetic South American husband of the dream had nothing at all to do with the quiet actuary she'd been settled with for nearly ten years, she found herself questioning her own motives for being with this actuary, as if all this time (as implied in her dream) she had only settled for the actuary as compensation for the boy she had refused when she was seventeen.

She began to think that the strangely remote and yet convincing mutual passion of the dream was in fact what had always been there in her heart and in his (however she might have been persuaded otherwise), and that it had only taken her subconscious this long to break through the quotidian insensibility of her life because of the layers and layers of self-denial and low self-esteem that had smoothed themselves over her seventeen-year-old self.

The only way to test this, she then told William, was to leave the actuary very suddenly, with no note, no explanation, nothing that could engage her over-conscientious feelings. She should set out on a methodical quest to track down the high school boy, who she was convinced was still single (since he had been so in the dream). Going to Singapore for a supposed extended visit to her brother was a perfect excuse, she said, because it had enabled a certain amount of her things to be removed from the house. The rest would have to be given up, but it was the only way to move forward. She wanted no dialogue about it with the actuary. For the first time in her life, she said, she was going to be true to her heart.

William's story finished there, which made everyone curious. Did the sister ever find the high school boy, and hadn't her dream actually indicated something different: that she should pursue the boy surreptitiously and yet stay with the actuary-cum-South American as her sister had advised? To these questions, William simply laughed. Of course it was a load of complete rubbish, he said. His sister had been an idiot to think of acting on such a flimsy thing as a dream. He had no idea whether she ever found the high school boy. For one thing, she was unlikely to be able to even recognise him, let alone still desire him (or he her) and the very most that could be accomplished would be a laying to rest of her lifetime of dreams about him (which perhaps would not have been such a mean achievement, but all the same quite absurd).

His sister had the idea, as she told William, that she wasn't actually going to try to speak to the boy when she found him. She knew, from idle discussions among old school friends, that he'd once worked for a large firm of architects in the city. She also had the email address that had been sent around to everyone as part of a list of email addresses after the last school reunion. She wasn't going to speak to him but simply send him an email. It was going to be a frank email, which would apologise for her way of refusing him all those years ago and explain how she had felt about him then. She would also apologise for the way she had blanked him many years later when, walking along a street, she had suddenly seen him (and presumably he her) and she had not known what to do. She would try accounting for the way the last time, at the very first school reunion – the one ten years after they had left school – she had done strange things to her hair in an effort to attract him.

It was at this point in his conversation with his sister that William had mused about the other sister. It was interesting, he'd said, that this other sister should have had such an intimate and sisterly role in the dream when in fact, as they both knew, she never showed her feelings, nor gave any indication of possessing human warmth. She was as cold as the coldest dead fish in the water near Hobart. While the dreaming sister might have wanted a more sisterly sister, the Hobart sister could in no way have ever managed to be that sister, and so it was a sure sign of the deceptive nature of the dream that this sister should have appeared exactly the opposite to how she really was.

William's story provoked a great deal of discussion, said Trude. Grace had heartily disagreed with William's cynicism, saying that sometimes a sense of conviction after a dream was all you ever had and perhaps his sister had been right to think that it was at last her subconscious desires speaking through. Monique then said she didn't know how anyone could be as pathetic as this sister of William. How on earth, at seventeen, could this sister have been so naïve? She herself certainly had not given a fuck for the opinions of her friends or anyone else and that was normal, she thought, for a teenager. With this, Jay had concurred. At seventeen, a girl is unlikely to be subtle, but stupid to that degree: it was totally beyond belief. Sure, she'd had a boyfriend when she was fourteen but anyone could see they were both only pretending at being boyfriend and girlfriend. Being gay made for situations like that when you were young. Grace then said that so much of relationships was a pretence anyway and she didn't see what everyone was getting so worked up about. There was not a single occasion in her life when she had thought she had been an authentic person. It was the nature of the post-post-post-modern world. Books were always being written and movies being made about people's supposed true feelings that were never even recognisable. We were all confused by these books and films. It could take you a lifetime to disentangle yourself from them.

These thoughts from Grace, Trude said, made everyone laugh and they seemed to forget about their disagreement. William, too, seemed to remember that someone was drawing him because he suddenly sat down on the nearest chair and made his back very straight.

There was a silence, Trude said, during which Sidney, the fat man, made one of his not-quite clearing of the throat noises. She turned a little towards him, so sorry did she feel for him, sitting alone there and yet still among the rest of them. The thrill that she was experiencing from the tacit agreement that she was someone who could draw well and should therefore be allowed to exhibit her skill made her at least begin to harbour indulgent feelings towards the fat man, who couldn't draw people but only fruit. She could see, or rather sense, that he was too shy to look up and so was looking at his hands, which he'd placed on either side of his now empty plate, the rounded backs of his hands the colour of uncooked sausages. It might have been nice of her, she remembered thinking, to say something to him. Just something small and about nothing in particular. Something about the meal perhaps, although she didn't know anything she could possibly say to him about it.

Monique and William had then got up again – William as if he was no longer aware that Trude had been drawing him, or else suddenly sick of being drawn, but now at least enjoying, even revelling, in being the acknowledged centre of attention. William wanted them to leave all the dirty plates for Dave. Dave got very bored in the evenings because hardly anyone ever ate at the pub. He also thought that, if they took the plates anywhere else, Dave would become convinced that they'd stolen them. They would hear him thumping around the corridors all evening, banging doors, tossing furniture, looking everywhere but the very obvious place they would have put the plates in their helpfulness. Dave would come to William then. William would hear him trembling at the door, his timid little knocks. Dave could get furious with William, they should understand, in the way that Dave never got furious with anybody else. Dave would not speak to William at such times. All William would have, he said, was his brother's trembling, as well as his terrible, very theatrical looks.

So that she might seem to have finished the drawing of William, which she hadn't banked on having to finish quite so abruptly, Trude said she had to use her fingers to simplify some of the shading. She then pushed the open cartridge pad to one side and leaned forward on the table in preparation for getting up. It was the easiest way to get herself out of her chair, since the chair she had chosen turned out to be rickety and too low. This was always the case, she said. She had noticed it everywhere since the accident. Nobody had adequate furniture. Nobody ever gave it a thought.

When he saw her trying to get out of the chair, William made a comment about how fit (meaning 'unfit', no doubt) she was. In some ways, this comment was reassuring. He had obviously not noticed how very hard it was for her to get around generally and therefore not thought that her difficulty could be attributed to anything more serious than a lack of fitness. Trude managed, or so she thought, a small smile of complicity or at least of acceptance. It was the only way to cope with people like William. People like William were always coming out with their sarcastic comments, hoping to get a laugh: if not from the person they were assaulting with their sarcasm, then any other person near that person. People like William had a particular way of interacting with the world. For example, he must have had a look at the picture she was doing of him but had chosen to say nothing about it. He could very easily have made a comment about how Trude was picturing him but instead he had chosen to make a comment at her expense about the state not so much of her health but of her worth as a person, because fitness was always measured in this moralising way.

William pretended to be not at all interested in the picture she'd drawn of him but the way he moved when he was up made her sure he was still enjoying being watched. There was a theatrical flourish to the way he grouped the dishes into the centre of the table and, when he walked over to the door and opened it briefly, the way his body turned towards her and the others (in the way of someone who has been trained to walk on a stage). William then said that his *cher* Dave had asked him expressly for the pleasure of entertaining the only gentleman in the group in his office that evening. It was Adelaide, wasn't it? Such an unusual name. It would be boring in Dave's office, though, he needed to warn their guest. All the ladders and paint tins and tools Dave seemed to need to get on top of his work, all of that cluttered up his older brother's office. There was hardly anywhere to sit. Dave had a television there, though. Most likely he'd be watching the tennis. There'd be the tennis on and Dave would have a bottle of something. William knew that Adelaide liked good times. He could see it in his face. Tennis and vodka most likely. Tennis and single malt if William could have picked it himself, but he knew there wouldn't be tennis and single malt but tennis and the very cheapest vodka or a bourbon with home-brand cola, little green olives from a supermarket jar, squares of pre-cut cheddar – perfect class, Adelaide needed to realise. They couldn't all know to choose the single malt. William said he had to apologise to the others, though. It was just a boy thing, he was afraid. Dave, he said, clammed up when he was around women. It would have to be the boy guest, their Adelaide, since none of them had thought to include any other boys in their party, only dykes.

The fat man got up and placed his hands on the back of the chair he'd been sitting in, or not so much his hands as his rigid, thick fingertips with their carefully pared nails. He was looking down in a way that made the swollen pink back of his neck very visible, Trude said. Trude thought he said something, although she didn't catch what it was.

William's voice was now strident and his sentences very fast. He seemed to be assuring the fat man that he would get into terrible trouble if he didn't go by Dave's office. There were his moods, William was saying. Dave was such a creature of his moods. William knew that his brother would think that he hadn't informed his guest, when he was expressly asked to remember to tell him (and any other appropriate guest, were there any available) once Adelaide (and anyone else he might have liked to talk to) had finished their meal. Dave liked talking, he was trying to assure the fat man, although Adelaide might never have thought so to hear him. Not a word from one minute to the next, and then Dave would be telling some story, or he'd be swearing, telling something that presumed his guest had heard the first part of a few minutes earlier. Dave just launched straight into the middle of his stories. But he relaxed with men like Adelaide. The other *gars* in the town – any of those under fifty who thought of coming to drink at Dave's pub – they were too skinny, too skimpy, too little in their heads, too nothing to talk about. All they ever thought about was their hairstyles and their CD collections and their organic carrot plantations (or hydroponic hash) and he had to assure Adelaide that there was nothing more disgusting to Dave than someone who only thought about such stupid *n'importe quoi* as hair and carrots and CDs, even hash. From the moment William had set eyes upon Adelaide, he could see that their guest wasn't someone who would bore their Dave with the number of albums he had in his CD collection, or his recent downloads (which came to as much). William thought their guest was above such superficial discussions as those that considered the shaving of sideburns or the amount of product (and didn't their guest love that chic word 'product'?) that might be necessary for that very sexy, very fetching oily-hair look they had: that sweaty Aragorn look, that look of men riding hard over the ranges but without all that riding hard over the ranges. William thought Adelaide was a man *au naturel*, he could see. *Un vrai homme sauvage.* Dave appreciated such things, William said, these little refinements, or, he should say, these telling restraints on their guest's refinements.

The fat man still had his hands on the back of his chair, Trude said. He looked as if he was wanting to back away, to get away from the table and from William, but due to the position of where William was standing and due, also, to the position of where Trude and Monique were standing, Trude saw that it would have been difficult for the fat man to escape from where he'd placed himself at the back of the chair he'd got out of.

William said that his friend shouldn't think that he was making fun of him when he, William, asked Adelaide to drop by with him at Dave's office as they left the bar. Dave was expecting him (William) as he was also expecting his very special guest. The tennis would go a long time into the night. There was no danger of that finishing too soon for their dropping by to be relevant. Dropping by was the only way to call on Dave. He was a terror for arrangements, although William thought he was also a terror for people who avoided his company. Why else, asked William, did Adelaide think he had to come all the way from Singapore (where he usually lived) to call on Dave? Weren't there simpler ways of sending money, or even of sending support to *un frère*? Dave had a genius for sending out over the seas, the way that whales could communicate with other whales, no matter which ocean they were swimming in. Dave was not going to eat Adelaide, William wanted to assure him. Dave was just a lonely man who liked his tennis and his television.

Trude said that the fat man's voice was weak when he tried to protest (just a single word of protest). He kept lifting his fingertips off the back of the chair and returning them to the place he'd taken them from. Jay and Grace took this moment to slip out of the room quietly, she noticed. It was disheartening, she said, after all of that for the evening to disintegrate in this way. For a moment – a short moment – she didn't care how this situation might have ended. She just wanted to leave. Her lower back, her pelvis and of course her leg were aching. She was feeling sick from the peculiar taste of congealed orange fat that had oozed from the sausages. It was a taste she associated with sausages that were bought in supermarkets rather than at the butcher, and on stiff polystyrene trays covered with plastic film.

Trude said that she might have left but instead she sat down again. She turned over the paper and decided to draw a new picture of William. This was then how, Trude told me, she really started drawing again – this time taking her art seriously (as Murray might have put it) – drawing the self-conscious gestures of this man William who was all the time building a performance against the presence of the fat man (as Monique had described it later). The more William began to enjoy himself with his performance

– as if conscious all the time that not only did he have an audience, but an infinity of spectators implied by the drawing – the more, Trude said, did she come to believe in her capacity to draw. She also began to believe that her drawing could be more than yet another drawing in a world already replete with images, the energy passing as it were through the subject to the artist (this passing through of energy being in itself a miracle, being what all the time she had ever wanted or desired from being able to draw). She did one image and then another, her lines becoming bolder and surer of themselves. You're a fabulous subject, she now felt like telling William. Have you ever been drawn or painted before? Have you ever been photographed?

Monique stayed silent, she remembered, and seemed only to be concentrating on watching the process of Trude's drawing. Trude could feel her there beside her, watching the unfurling of each drawing from the perspective of the artist, as Monique put it later. Trude now worked fast, filling one after another of the pages in her cartridge pad, each image becoming surer than the last. Monique was impressed, she then said, and kept saying that Trude had really caught his energy. They were quite some pictures, she was saying. She wished she could draw even half so well.

Trude said that she drank in these comments, so happy was she with what was happening to her drawing. It was as if she had now struck oil, she said, as if she had at last found the weakest part of the earth's crust and it was hers to gather all the liquid that emerged, this liquid no longer seeping pathetically, but welling up, flooding as from the richest store of oil that had ever been discovered. She became even more daring with the charcoal: now a single line of left-hand silhouette, now one page inhabited entirely by the junction of hair, collared neck and shirt creases. Now one hand rising huge, the pale head small as a memory in the distance. Would you ever consider, Trude planned on asking William – would you ever allow me to use you for a whole series of pictures? I want to do something with these sketches (the word 'something' already confirming to her that she was at last becoming an artist).

And all the time, of course, the fat man had just stood there. There were two fat men in the room, said Trude, but she had only drawn one of them. It even occurred to her as she drew that switching to drawing Sidney in this situation might have been cruel. She could easily have drawn Sidney, the way she had drawn Monique on the table. She could have done him as a warmer, as a 'one minuter', just capturing the way he stood there at the chair. One long line around this way. The chair back coming out of him as if it was joined to his waist. It was all she was doing with William, she could see. She was drawing at the edge of her consciousness. She rode with each impression and each impression then took on a life of its own. William was grotesque in her drawings and she began to wonder whether his seeing that grotesqueness whenever he glanced over at what she was doing was only encouraging him to say crueller and crueller things to Sidney, the fat man – absurd, foul and humiliating things to the fat man – and the fat man just kept staring at his hands on the chair back, his thick, pink, soft hands curling around the wood. He had the look of someone who was waiting for a particular lot of traffic to pass down the street before he crossed, as if all his life there had always been this lot of noisy and dangerously fast or unpredictable traffic passing down the very street he had to cross every day of his life.

The whole time William hounded the fat man, eventually becoming lewd with his descriptions of his brother and his insinuations about both of them, Trude found that she was drawing more and more daring and bold images of William. And yet all the time she was wishing she could switch and draw Sidney instead. Monique was fascinated by her drawings of William and it reminded Trude of when she used to draw the teachers at school – making the glasses of one as large as Dame Edna's, the beard of another go down as far as his knees, the strange stork-stepping of another teacher cross an entire double page of her maths exercise book – because it was only such exaggerations which caught the attention of her classmates. It was how it was, she said. It was the only reason she had ever drawn.

It was only ever the attention of her classmates that she desired, she realised. There was nothing better than being surrounded by her classmates as she drew a teacher who they all despised or at least very readily recognised.

Nothing could go wrong during such a moment; the pencil would draw, it would seem, all on its own. There was something magic about this willing of the drawing before an audience. All the time there would be the half realisation that it was all a sham and, if she thought about it too closely, the drawing would collapse into a hopeless tangle of indecipherable or – which was worse – inaccurate lines. And so all the time she would be holding her breath or taking, at the most, very shallow sips of air, as if to breathe freely would be to frighten the magic away, this magic that she had commandeered for herself. It was the meaning of the door sliding shut in front of her, she decided. All this creativity was what had been released in her mind. Her direction in life was clear. She no longer felt any dread about the possible negative interpretations of the sign of the door, only complete happiness and a conviction that everything was going to turn out as it should. She had never, ever, felt so happy, so completely connected with herself as she had felt then with those drawings of William during his ranting.

Things faltered, though, Trude said, when she at last got enough courage to interrupt him as he spoke. She knew she had to do this: to take up her dream in both hands at last (her dream to become an artist) and direct it for herself for the first time in her life. This being decided, she perhaps wasn't so careful in the timing of when she spoke. She was so caught up in her own excitement, she must have chosen an awkward time, because when eventually Trude said she wanted to 'do something' with the images she was making, and asked whether he minded that they were of him, William just looked at her for a moment and then continued with what he had been saying but with such an expression of disgust on his face that she might have asked him whether she could touch an intimate part of his body.

It was not long after she said that she wanted to do something with the images she'd done of him that William left the room without saying one word more either to the fat man or to Monique or to herself. For a while, Trude said, both she and Monique had just expected him to walk back into the room, either carrying something or wiping his wet hands on his trousers as he walked, but he didn't. For a while, she then just kept on touching up some of the drawings, with Monique making a comment about whether she liked a particular drawing or thought it needed more work, and as they were both looking through all the pictures Trude had made, the fat man left the room too. Soon all there was, she said, was just the pictures and Monique and herself and a table of dirty dishes.

Trude looked at Monique now, but Trude said she no longer felt she wanted to capture the essentials in the other woman's face. It might have been one of those terrible moments, she now told me: one of those terrible moments when you realise that you've been acting like an idiot, like a fool, but she had to tell herself that what had happened inside her, in her own heart, should not be so dismissed and pushed to the side. All her life there had been opportunities to ride the wave of her convictions. Several times as a child she had become convinced at a particular moment that she had been born to be nothing else but an artist. Each of these moments was very clear in her mind. They were mostly moments when she was looking out over a landscape or looking through a window onto a quiet street beneath. Too soon after each of these occasions, she said, she had let the clutter and disorder of ordinary life intrude on her thoughts. She was also, she thought, too easily misled by signs that were seemingly unpropitious but were nothing more than irritating events. With the emptying of the room they'd all been sitting in, she might have easily forgotten the new-found conviction about her own abilities, but she made herself ignore the distraction. It was the only way.

That night, Trude said, she didn't sleep well. It was hard to be sure that she even slept at all, so churned and tiring were her many dreams that seemed as much about herself trying to sleep against the roar of ideas as they were actual dreams in themselves. The next morning, she was a little late coming downstairs with her bags. There had been no mention of break-fast, nor of any time they should leave, and so she wasn't sure whether they were going to be eating at the hotel. Dave had met her halfway down the stairs and, without offering to help her the rest of the way to the bottom, proffered the unasked-for information that William had gone out for his usual walk along the river.

Nobody ate anything at all that morning. The others had gathered in the same little room behind the bar, all their bags lined up in front of them and all as dour, Trude said, as any lot of travellers with a long way to go still in front of them. It was extraordinary how quickly their previous enthusiasm had vanished. It was just as well that she had forced herself to ignore the seemingly depressing end to a very important evening, and also the discouraging absence of the main subject himself, because this probably allowed Monique, she thought (the moment that someone suggested that they go out for a coffee at least), to bring up the fact that Trude had done these really interesting pictures of William, and so Trude, to her great happiness and pride, brought them out of her bag.

The response was not as great as she had hoped. So intense and convincing had been her dreams the night before that she had almost imagined the very words that the others would say about them – words that, if few, might have confirmed her in her feelings about her work – but of course the reality was a little different. She didn't let that bother her, though. Mostly in her life she had been too thin-skinned to be serious about her art. It wasn't good to be thin-skinned. Nobody got anywhere by being too thin-skinned. An important thing had happened to her the night before, and so she made herself ignore anything that could dampen her conviction. She was at last ready to take her art seriously and she knew in which direction she had to go. No one could take that from her, Trude said to me, now that she knew.

In fact, it wasn't too bad because, although Jay said very little about the pictures when she saw them – and she might at least have said that they were interesting – Grace went through all of them and laid them out along the tables in the room in a kind of sequence, and said that Trude should really get an exhibition together – that she really had enough material for an exhibition. Grace hadn't exactly said whether she liked them or not, simply that there were enough works there for an exhibition. But it was sufficient, Trude said. That little was sufficient, and it was then that the fat man spoke up and suggested that place where she eventually had that exhibition (had

I heard about the exhibition? she now asked).

The fat man said that he had these neighbours who ran a small space in the front of their house for exhibitions. It had been these neighbours who had encouraged him to go on the art workshop in the first place, because they could see that otherwise he was never going to give himself a go. He had once told them how much he had loved drawing as a child, although it was painting that mostly interested him. Round things and still things had been what had interested him, the strange, inaccessible thingness of things. He had no idea how it was that these neighbours had remembered this little scrap he had told them, but they had asked him along with some other neighbours to the openings of their exhibitions. They hadn't been big name exhibitions (in fact he rather thought that the exhibitions were just showings of some of the work of their friends), but there had always been one or two pictures in the exhibitions that had particularly interested him. It would please him to look very carefully at them. Sometimes he had even considered buying one or two of these pictures that had caught his fancy, but he had always told himself that there would have been no point buying any of the pictures, since he lived alone. These neighbours of his, he said, were very encouraging of him, even pushing him hard to go on this Getaway Art Workshop – saying things like you have the money and what else are you going to spend it on if you don't spend it on yourself.

All in all, or so he told Trude, these neighbours of his would be good people to start with if she wanted to have an exhibition. He himself was never going to do anything worth hanging. In fact, the whole time at the art workshop he had realised that it was useless trying to pick up on what he had done all those years ago. Perhaps he had expected that the feeling he had had for the things he used to paint might still have been there, waiting for him – untapped, so to speak – until the moment he started drawing or painting again. He had gone through the motions, he said, of drawing at the workshop, working mostly on what he remembered he had done all those years ago when he was a boy. What the tutors had said meant nothing to him. He had no intention of being creative or becoming an artist.

He only wanted to find that quiet space again, that quiet space that kept getting away from him the closer he came to it. All the words he had picked up during the workshop – words like 'blocking in the colour' and 'defining the space' – all this had got in the way, he found, of the very faint, very slightest of sensations, the very edge of the feelings he had once had when he tried to get the quietness of a pear on a plate. In fact, he had realised that in his life, in his little house, he had always made a space that intersected with the feelings of love – that was how he now defined it – for the quietness of a pear or an orange in his childhood. The moment he closed the front door behind him, the quietness of his house opened out to him. He was not an artist, he realised, and he certainly wasn't creative. He had learned something, perhaps, about the way of pulling out lots of different colours from a single coloured object and he might have continued wanting to do this if it had answered anything for him.

His neighbours had meant well, but they really hadn't any idea what they were talking about. All the same, he continued, they would be the ones to give a new artist a try. One of them was in advertising and the other had once been a teacher. This had been the dream of the teacher, to have her own gallery. Her own works were odd – boats made out of African chestnut cases and panels of paperbark – and he never could see anything much in either the boats or the panels, although the panels got him wanting to lay his cheeks against them (or perhaps the backs of his hands).

That was all the fat man said, and as he talked he didn't look at the drawings, but at the table in front of him. He just offered this bit about his neighbours and their gallery – this very useful information whose details Trude wrote down right away – and then he shut up.

None of the travellers from the art camp ended up seeing William again before they left on the next coach to Sydney. After they all got back from their coffee up the street, Monique asked once or twice whether William had come back from his walk along the river, but Dave would either say he didn't know or would look straight through her to the place on the wall where he had been working on regluing some panelling.

It was difficult, Trude told me, because everyone had just seen what a huge amount of drawing she had done, and they were all urging her to get a show together. It was difficult because, although she had asked William at the end of the evening whether he minded her 'doing something' with the sketches she had done of him, he had never actually replied to the question. By implication, she thought, he had seemed pleased she was drawing him but at the same time, she knew, it would be unethical to go ahead with an exhibition that centred on someone very identifiable but who hadn't in fact given their permission to be shown.

When she voiced these concerns to Monique, all Monique had said was that she thought William was just someone who would love to be the subject of an exhibition. She only needed to send him an invitation, in a way that would indicate that he was the honoured guest. Men like William were only ever interested in being the centre of attention. In fact, Monique thought, if Trude hadn't mainly drawn William, he would very likely have felt insulted. Besides, he was a cool guy. He had been everywhere and done a great many things. Monique then said that, surely, Trude didn't actually need to name the person she had been drawing, and anyway, she thought Trude could do something adventurous with the sketches. They could become wholly unrecognisable, and what was more, since there had been two big men in the room at the time she had been drawing, there was no way, if William ended up being touchy about the matter, that he could prove that the draw-ings weren't of Sidney rather than himself. Sure, William's shirt had been unbuttoned a little further down than Sidney's, but really, apart from that, there was no other way anyone could begin to guess which big man had been the subject of the drawings. Even Grace, Monique said, had asked her who the drawings were of, and she at least had seen both William and Sidney, even if she hadn't actually been present when most of the drawings were done. Monique then said that she would be the only one who might know any differently, and perhaps the models themselves, and if William was at all concerned that he might be the subject of a whole exhibition of images that was out of his hands, well, it was up to him to say he wasn't happy, wasn't it, rather than taking himself off for a fucking walk.

All the way back to Sydney in the coach, Trude said that she hadn't wanted to talk. There weren't very many seats left in the coach when they were picked up and so the five of them had had to sit separately, which made it easier not to offend anyone by her wish to be silent. There was something, she said, about the contrast between the clarity of the details of cars and the wedges of blue and white sliced in diagonals by electricity wires (and soon the rustling yellow and the finer wire of fences) – something about the contrast between the clarity and continuity of the outside, and the grey, layered nylon silhouettes of the window frame and curtains inside the bus that reminded Trude of the excitement of 'the revelation', as she now put it, of the sliding door the previous evening and everything that had followed on from it.

In her bag she had the drawings – the beginnings of her new and decisive life as an artist – the evidence that she had already begun that life and, thus far (only a day), had lived it entirely in keeping with her new reality. Her vision, she now saw, had grown more sensitised. She was looking at everything as though through a real artist's eyes. If it had taken her all her life thus far to realise the artist potential in herself, she said, she knew it would be more than made up for by the quality of her artwork, as evidenced by the responses that morning to the drawings she had done of William. Some artists, she had become convinced, might take half their lives to discover the truth of their calling. It would not make her a packet, but she no longer – due to the payout from the accident – had to worry about such business as earning her own keep.

And so it was in this way that her thoughts came once more around to Murray who, all this time, had been unaware that she had stayed the extra night up the coast. But even then, said Trude, the elation of her thoughts about art very easily cancelled the uneasiness she felt about having failed to call him. It had been so long since she'd had to inform someone or other of her whereabouts. When she had been single, she had never appreciated such freedom. All those years, she thought, she might have broken free and become an artist – all those years of never having to let someone else know where she was had been wasted until the moment of her accident. It had taken the accident, she now realised, to shake something of real sense into her. And it had been Murray, after all – that angel of the accident – who had persuaded her to go on the Getaway Art Workshop, which had, inadvertently (although miraculously), changed her life forever. It had been the combination of her mother and Murray who had virtually forced her to go on the art workshop which had not interested her in the least, and yet because of the art workshop – and because of the accident of events since that art workshop – she now knew that she had no other choice than the one of being an artist.

When she got back to Sydney, Trude said, it astonished her how quickly this new decision about her art began to affect everything else. First there was the problem of Murray and of whether to continue living with him in his house. Trude said that she'd been both touched and irritated by his concern after those few days away. The moment she climbed back into his car when she arrived (nearly an hour later, as she'd had to ring him first from the coach station), she felt his pale protuberant eyes fasten on her, his suppressed anger at her lack of communication seeping into everything he said, and she knew that it was impossible to continue to draw as she had drawn at the pub so long as she had to justify herself to him every minute of the day.

She proceeded with the exhibition, for no other reason than that Monique, with whom she had exchanged phone numbers, had kept ringing her up about it, even offering to help with the framing. Murray was supportive too, said Trude. He was extremely supportive. I had to understand, Trude said, that this supportiveness of Murray was a way of being in the world she had never experienced before and would perhaps never experience again. She wished she could describe her relationship with Murray better, only she was afraid she would sound cynical and unlovable (and she hated cynics). Everything about the lucky chance of her relationship with Murray was recognisable, she said, from books she had read and films she had seen.

She went on with the exhibition with the full support of Murray. It had been quick to arrange and the opening had been one of those balmy evenings when the crowd spills out onto the quiet of the footpath. Monique had come to the opening, and so had Jay and Grace. William had never replied to the letter she had sent to the pub and so, when it came to it, she had decided to fudge the identity of the man she had drawn – calling the images now only man 1, man 2 and so on – and when the gallery owners asked her whether she had been drawing Sidney, their friend, she said that she might have, although she hadn't wanted to say.

Just as she was unable to know how exactly she felt about Murray and the imperative of her art, she also found it difficult to know whether it mattered that she had lied about the identity of the figure. Sidney hadn't come to the exhibition opening and she hadn't been able to find out why. The gallery owners had thought he was coming – they had only seen him the other day. He often looked in at the windows as he passed by on his way to work in the mornings. Even in the evenings – if he was late home from work – they would occasionally see him stop at one of the pieces in the window. They would look out for him, they said. Very obviously he had been an important inspiration. He was that sort of person, they said. On a first meeting you might think him a little more stupid than he was, but that was only because he didn't push himself forwards like most people did. It took time to get to know a gem like Sidney. Any day now, they said, he'd probably call around and talk endlessly (and fruitlessly) of buying one of the pieces he liked.

All in all, Trude said, she thought she'd had enough of showing her art in public. She'd ridden the wave of opportunity as it arose, but she hadn't been happy with how it turned out. There was a difference in being excited with your own drawing and trying to interest other people in your drawings as objects (in that whole exhibition thing).

She could still see a role for exhibitions. Without exhibitions it would be hard to find out about the world of art, and therefore nearly impossible to see yourself and your work in relation to it. But after her own exhibition, despite selling more than half of the works, she had been very depressed. It had been her first solo art show and she should have enjoyed it but instead she had spent all her time talking too fast to people and telling lies about the pictures she had done: not only lies about the subject of the drawings, but lies about what all the drawings had meant in combination, as an exhibition.

After a glass or two of wine, she'd grown detached from what she was saying to people. She could see our mother over on one side of the room. I should have been there, she said. I would have enjoyed listening to how our mother had talked: to the way she pronounced that word 'exhibition' (those indistinct syllables, as if she had already grown tired of Trude's success). In the end, Trude had decided, her art had nothing to do with exhibitions and nothing to do with other people. It had been great reliving, as she put it, those titillating moments of being the centre of even a small attention. It had been great, that is, until only a few minutes into it.

At the pub after the art workshop, she had assumed it was the only way to be an artist and in this she had been wrong. Out of all the people she had met on that workshop and at the pub afterwards, it had only been the fat man, Sidney, who might have been able to understand what she was now thinking. He wasn't an artist, but she thought he still had an idea of what it was that was gripping her about art. She had given up her interest in figures, she said. There was something else she wanted to draw, but she hadn't quite discovered what it was. It could take months, perhaps, even years to discover what it was she needed to make. She had to empty herself out first, empty herself out until she found out who she was.

When Trude finished talking, it had grown dark. Still, comparatively speaking, the sky was very light and very clear.

Although I was unaware it had grown cold, I found myself so hunched up where I was sitting at the plastic table on the balcony that my elbows had wedged themselves into my sides. It was only then, while almost immobilised by the cold and my passivity – a passivity I now realised was nothing but a hatred that was growing progressively staler the longer I stayed – I suddenly remembered that, as well as the book and the flowers I had brought for her, our mother had sent along a bag of newspaper clippings that she thought Trude might be interested in: in fact, her words were that she knew Trude never bothered reading the paper, and there were a few things that she had found on various topics such as rehabilitation and portrait painting and the dangers of living right on a main road (as she was) that she thought Trude shouldn't ignore. She had also sent me over with a bag of mandarins that were only just then coming into season. Trude was probably only eating awful pub food and it was important, our mother had told me, that I tried encouraging her to eat something better for her health. Trude never listened to her, our mother kept telling me, and she would probably go to her grave trying to spite her mother all the way, so it was important that I did something to help her to change her life for the better. Just encouraging her to eat some of the mandarins would be at least something, our mother had said. The way to do it, she told me, was to take out one of them and eat it with her. It is hard to resist a mandarin when someone is eating one in front of you. That was what I should do, she had told me, and then after that I could talk about helping her to move somewhere else and about how she should consider trying to contact that poor man Murray. The mandarin first and the suggestion afterwards.

Such were my directions, Remi (should I ever get around to sending this journal to you: you whose surprise at my sudden decision to leave France I can only now begin to understand).

You see, it wasn't that I consciously refused to be party to my mother's directions, nor determined, out of my own spite, to withhold something from Trude (something which might even have been mildly useful to her). Perhaps, had the directions and my spite – and the despair that was growing inside me: that all the time I thought I was doing something for my self by coming back to Australia and reconnecting with my family and especially with Trude, I was in fact only submitting to an expectation (theirs) that by reconnecting with my family and with Trude I would be solving something for my self, an expectation of solving something that had nothing whatsoever to do with me and everything to do with what my family and especially Trude were telling themselves, that they couldn't help but continue telling themselves – had all this not interfered with my thinking, I might have thought to warn Trude that Charlene and Dennis had been in regular touch with our mother; that they had agreed to terminate their arrangement with Trude by the end of the month and had accepted monetary compensation for terminating the arrangement.

I might also have got out one of those mandarins of my own accord while we were still sitting at that table because I hadn't eaten anything for hours and had grown quite hungry. Or so I thought afterwards in the train.

www.ingramcontent.com/pod-product-compliance
Lightning Source LLC
Chambersburg PA
CBHW030529020726
47494CB00004B/1282